It was an enormous bat.

She turned again toward the door.

And it swooped down out of the sky. Instinctively she flung up her hands and felt the brush of fur. She stumbled toward the stairs and half fell.

It was on her again. Huge wings brushed her face. In the light from the entrance she saw a face pressing close to hers.

A mouth opened. A row of needle-sharp teeth . . .

It was an enormous bat.

"NOOOOOOOO!" she screamed.

Terrifying thrillers by Diane Hoh:

Funhouse
The Accident
The Invitation
The Train
The Fever

Nightmare Hall: The Silent Scream
Nightmare Hall: The Roommate
Nightmare Hall: Deadly Attraction
Nightmare Hall: The Wish
Nightmare Hall: The Scream Team
Nightmare Hall: Guilty
Nightmare Hall: Pretty Please
Nightmare Hall: The Experiment
Nightmare Hall: The Night Walker
Nightmare Hall: Sorority Sister
Nightmare Hall: Last Date
Nightmare Hall: The Whisperer
Nightmare Hall: Monster
Nightmare Hall: The Initiation
Nightmare Hall: Truth or Die
Nightmare Hall: Book of Horrors
Nightmare Hall: Last Breath
Nightmare Hall: Win, Lose or Die
Nightmare Hall: The Coffin
Nightmare Hall: Deadly Visions
Nightmare Hall: Student Body
Nightmare Hall: The Vampire's Kiss

NIGHTMARE HALL

The Vampire's Kiss

DIANE HOH

SCHOLASTIC INC.
New York Toronto London Auckland Sydney

ISBN 0-590-25089-2

12 11 10 9 8 7 6 5 4 3 2 1   5 6 7 8 9/9 0/0

Printed in the U.S.A.   01

First Scholastic printing, April 1995

NIGHTMARE HALL

The Vampire's Kiss

First Scholastic printing, April 199

Prologue

He had never been so powerful. So strong. So sure of himself. He'd never felt so good.

He stood up dizzily. The world swung around him, the dark and velvet world.

It was nighttime. He'd been asleep for a long, long time.

Maybe he'd slept his life away.

But that was over now.

Something moved in the underbrush. The faintest sound, inaudible to the human ear. But he wasn't cursed with mere human hearing anymore.

He knew what the sound was, what made it. His eyes glinted in the darkness and he could see the shape of the animal in the deep shadows where it thought itself safe.

Instinctively, he raised one hand and called it forth.

It came, creeping and cowering, repulsive and low.

An enormous rat.

Fearlessly he reached out and gripped its throat in fingers of iron. He raised it up. It hung limply, resignedly in his hands. The only sign of life was the glint of its wicked eyes.

"I could kill you," he told it softly. "I could drink your blood."

The rat twitched. Abruptly he dropped it, already tired of the game. What was the blood of a rat? He wanted more.

"Go," he said wearily and it scurried away.

He heard it then. A human heartbeat nearby. A human was walking down the dark path. A foolish human.

In an instant he had furled his coat around himself, had become a bat and flown up into the darkness. He circled there and saw it. A beautiful human.

A lovely human.

It would give him a few minutes' pleasure. Perhaps, in return, he would let it live . . . Forever.

myna bird or something. Or what about tha

Chapter 1

"Tall deuce dark cinnamon whipped, tall skinny plain, one house cake."

"Are you ordering a guy or a coffee for the customers?" cracked Crystal Avon, coming up behind Janie Curtis.

"Ha, ha," answered Janie. To Norton, the owner-manager of the popular coffee bar Morte par Chocolat, at one edge of Salem University's campus, she said, "Got all that?"

"Yep." Norton was a man of few words and swift actions. He was already assembling the double shot of espresso with a dash of milk, a topping of whipped cream and a dash of cinnamon, the tall double espresso with skim milk and nothing else, and the slice of Death by Chocolate cake that was the house specialty and namesake of Morte par Chocolat.

Crystal pushed back the shock of silver-blonde hair that she wore in a tousled, moussed disarray, rolled her deceptively innocent silver-green eyes and said, "Has this been a busy night, or *what*? I can hardly wait to go home and put my weight on something else besides my feet."

"Got a boyfriend coming over?" Janie shot back.

"*Good* one." Crystal flashed her good-natured, slightly mischievous smile at Janie and then said, "Speaking of tall orders, check out the guy in the back left corner booth. But be cool about it, okay? 'Cause there isn't much he hasn't missed since he sat down tonight."

Propping herself against the wall next to the order window, Janie flipped through her notepad and glanced casually in the direction Crystal had indicated. For a moment, her heart stopped.

For a moment time stood still . . . .

He'd always had a habit of stillness. It was one of the first things she'd liked about him — the way he didn't show off, didn't act up, didn't try to be the center of attention. Later, toward the end, although she never admitted it, she'd wondered if the stillness wasn't a waiting, a listening. As if all the focus of his long, lean body had always been on what was to come.

As if he knew he was going to die and leave her alone after all . . .

"Janie, I said take a look at the guy, not memorize him!" Crystal gave Janie a nudge. At the same moment Norton slammed his hand down on the order ready bell and said, "Order!"

With a supreme effort, Janie tore her eyes from the figure crouched over his coffee in the back corner booth. She picked up the order and slid it onto the tray. She pasted a smile on her face and walked to her table.

Janie was a good waitress. A pro, even after such a short time. She served the orders now without a hitch, brought extra napkins, refilled two cups of homestyle, as plain American coffee was called at Morte par Chocolat, collected a check, and made change. During the whole time, she smiled and nodded and acted as if she were in complete control.

But she wasn't. Inside, her heart was racing, her stomach churning. She felt sick. She thought she was going to faint.

Janie made her way toward Crystal, who now sat at the end of the counter where the waiters and waitresses hung out whenever they had a minute off their feet.

"Is he still there?" Janie asked.

"Who? Oh. No. He's gone." Crystal's voice sharpened with curiosity. "Why? Did you recognize him? He's an ex who did you wrong?"

That made Janie smile. It was one of the

things she liked about Crystal. She was, like her name, crystal clear. Predictable. Straightforward.

And unabashedly curious about what she suspected was Janie's "dark secret."

Only it wasn't a dark secret, just a tragic one. One that Janie had no intention of sharing with Crystal or anyone at the cafe. Because here, where no one knew what had happened, where no one knew where she came from, where no one knew about her past, there were no painful reminders. Here, she was just Janie, another Salem student who needed the extra money. Another waitress who had to hustle to make her work schedule, her class schedule, her social life all fit together.

"I never saw him before in my life," Janie said at last, allowing herself to look toward the dark corner where the figure had been sitting. "But you're right, Crystal. He did remind me, for a moment, of someone I once knew. An — ex."

Satisfied, Crystal said, "It happens to me, too. I think I've gotten over somebody and bam! there he is. Or someone who looks enough like him to be his twin brother . . . and you know what? I usually end up falling for the same type all over again."

"Gotta break that habit," Janie said. She

jumped off the stool as two earnest-looking girls and their dates came through the door and headed for one of her tables. "The best thing is to stay busy and learn to forget." Or at least stay busy, she thought bitterly. Because she would never forget.

Never.

"Forget? Ha!" Crystal said. "If I could remember anything for more than two seconds except the last guy who done me wrong, I wouldn't be a full-time waitress and a part-time student. Salem would've made me an academic scholarship offer I couldn't refuse."

Janie smiled bitterly as she walked smoothly, efficiently, toward the table. Good old Crystal. Inside, Janie was dying. But thanks to Crystal's chatter, on the outside, Janie was in control.

At least for now.

The book slid lower and lower. Her eyes drooped. And then she was asleep. Dreaming.

"Lucas?"

He turned, in that slow, measured way he had. But she could tell, just the same, that he was excited, quivering with anticipation. That he was glad to see her.

"Lucas, is it really you?"

He nodded. He opened his arms.

All the pain, all the grief, all the loneliness of the preceding months fell away. It had all been a nightmare. A bad dream, just as she had known it was.

"Oh, Lucas," she gasped. She flung herself against him, reached up to kiss him.

His kiss was as passionate and as sweet as she remembered. A kiss she could never forget. A kiss like no one else's. I could be dying, she thought happily, and know it was Lucas I was kissing. Know it was Lucas who was holding me.

He pulled back slightly, to press his lips against her hair. She nestled against the hollow of his throat.

And felt the wetness.

Blood. Her whole body stiffened. It was the blood. The blood that had covered his throat when she'd found him. The heartsblood, the lifeblood . . .

"No," she gasped, trying to free herself. She jerked back despite Lucas's inarticulate sound of protest.

But there was no blood. His throat was smooth and firm and strong.

"Janie?" he whispered at last, staring down at her.

And she realized it wasn't blood she had felt,

but tears. All the tears she hadn't cried since that awful night. . . .

The crash awoke her. Her history book had slipped free from her fingers and off the narrow dorm bed to the floor. She jerked upright, raising her hands to her face.

But she wasn't crying. She'd never cried. She only cried in her dreams.

That's why I cry, she thought. Because I have to wake up. That's the nightmare.

"Don't you ever sleep?" said a familiar voice as the door of the dorm room opened.

Hastily Janie bent over to retrieve her book. When she straightened up, she felt some of the color returning to her face.

She smiled and answered lightly, "Don't you ever study?"

"Honey, how long have you known me?"

"Since kindergarten," said Janie.

"Well then, that should answer your question." Susanne Delacorte stalked dramatically over to her bed across the room from Janie and dropped down with a sigh. "But I guess I'm gonna have to start. I don't think I can slide through Salem on looks and charm alone."

Janie laughed and shook her head. "This is me you're talking to, remember? Your best friend since forever. I know how smart you are.

What I don't understand and never will is why you pretend not to be."

Susanne looked all around, then raised a finger to her lips. "I'll tell you, but you must promise never to tell *another living soul*."

"I promise," said Janie solemnly. "Cross my heart and hope to die."

Susanne lowered her head so that a wedge of chin-length, chestnut brown hair fell across her face. Peering out from behind it, she said, "I act — dumb — because I like for people to be *unpleasantly* surprised."

Janie burst out laughing and Susanne joined her, looking pleased.

Then Susanne stopped and looked at Janie. "You know, it's nice to hear you laugh. It's been a long time."

Janie felt the laughter drain out of her. Damn Susanne! She was referring to Lucas, to Lucas's death, of course. But why did she have to remind Janie of it?

Susanne realized her mistake instantly, but she refused to be contrite. "Okay, so I'm tactless. But I knew Lucas, too, Janie. I'm the one who introduced you to each other, remember? In fact, I was on a date with him when he met you . . ."

"You said you were just friends," said Janie quickly, hoping to change the subject.

Susanne waved her hand dismissively and went on. "You've got to mourn him, get over him, go on with your life."

"I am going on with my life! I came to Salem didn't I? We're rooming together, just like we planned on doing, aren't we?"

"Big whoop," Susanne said. "You came to Salem. You study, work, eat, and sleep, maybe, sometimes. You never go out. You never have fun. You haven't even made any new friends."

"I have. I've made friends at the cafe."

Again Susanne waved her hand dismissively. She didn't understand why Janie worked at the cafe if she didn't need the money. Janie suspected that Susanne was a bit of a snob, that she looked down on the students who had to work to help pay their way through school. She couldn't understand that for Janie, it wasn't the money, it was the time. That working passed the time. And at Morte par Chocolat, Janie was just another waitress, just another student grinding her way through Salem U, nothing more. It felt good.

But she could never explain that to Susanne. Had given up trying. "I never was as outgoing as you were, Susanne. Never. Even before . . . everything."

"You can't even say his name, can you?" Susanne put her hands on her hips. "This is *not* healthy, Janie. I'm worried about you. You're going to go on never crying and never mourning and never dealing with what happened and pretending that you are strong enough to take it and staying shut off from the world and one day . . . one day, you're just going to snap."

For a moment, Janie looked steadily at Susanne. Susanne looked back, her hazel eyes fixed unblinkingly on Janie's blue ones. Eerily, unexpectedly, Janie thought of the stranger in the restaurant who had reminded her, for one fleeting moment, of Lucas. It was that instant in the restaurant, she realized, that had brought on the nightmare, had shown her just how vulnerable she was.

Maybe Susanne was right, more right than Janie wanted to admit. Maybe Janie wasn't getting over Lucas after all.

Janie looked away first. I wish I could sleep forever, she thought. I wish that I had died with Lucas.

But she hadn't. She'd been late to their date, late because her parents had forbidden her to see Lucas. They'd never liked Lucas. He wasn't good enough for her, they said. She needed to go out into the world, go to college, meet other people. She was too young to be so seriously involved with anyone. Too young to really know what it meant to love someone.

So she'd had to sneak out to meet Lucas that night. And she'd been late. And he'd waited for her, alone on that dark corner at the edge of the park. She could imagine, had imagined him waiting as she hurried toward their meeting. He'd be standing there, still as a statue, his hands deep in the pockets of the worn black leather jacket he always wore. He'd be wearing a white T-shirt and black jeans and boots and he'd look like a long, lean shadow there — except that he would be darker, more substantial, less movable.

Until he saw her. And then he would turn, and smile, and she would run into his arms.

But he hadn't been there. She'd been running, breathlessly, skimming through the night as if she could fly, feeling curiously at home. Rounding the corner, she'd already begun to smile.

Then she stopped. Walked slowly forward. Leaned over the dark shape sprawled on the sidewalk by the side of the park.

"Luke," she said. "Lucas? It's me. Janie. Wake up, Luke."

Of course he hadn't. He never would again. He lay there, staring up with sightless eyes at the pattern of branches woven in the trees that leaned down above him. A jagged gash of blood across his throat glistened blackly in the dim glow of the streetlight on the far corner.

The night had been so still. So still. But not as still as Lucas. Lucas, who had practiced such calm, such reserve, such measured motion, had achieved the ultimate stillness, the final silence.

"Lucas, wake up," she whispered, kneeling beside him. But he never would. Never again for all eternity . . .

"Janie," said Susanne, her voice sounding frightened.

Janie looked up.

Susanne looked quickly away, as if she had seen something that she didn't like.

"What?" Janie said harshly. "What do you want me to do? Lucas is dead, Susanne. *Dead.* Gone. Buried. I'll never see him again. I know that. I'll live my whole life without him.

"See? I can say it. I can understand it. I understand it better than you or anyone thinks.

"Lucas is dead. And there's nothing anyone can do or say that will ever change it."

Chapter 2

"He's heeere," whispered Crystal out of the side of her mouth.

"He who?" Janie frowned down at her order pad. Being a waitress was ruining her handwriting. It had gotten so bad she couldn't even read it herself.

The order bell dinged, and Crystal began loading her tray.

"The guy who was here the other night. Mr. Looks-Like-Your-Ex-Heartbreaker," said Crystal.

Janie snorted. "Sounds like the title of a bad country song, Crys." But after she'd read the order to Norton, she allowed herself to turn and slowly scan the room.

It was a weekend night, and a slow one. The Salem women's basketball team was on an away trip; the Salem men's team had a game at the gym that night. The crowd — and the tips — would pick up later, after the game. Then the cafe would fill with basketball fans, along with a mix of night owls that included not only the students with late-night library complexions but others who stayed up late to pursue other, more decadent interests.

But the crowd was sparse now, and he was easy to spot in the back corner booth. Crystal had dubbed the booth, which was the most secluded and dark of the booths, the second-date booth. She maintained that if a first date went well, on the second date you took that booth and went for the romance.

But he was there alone again. Janie steadied herself for the pain of remembrance, that twisting knife in the heart that had come so unexpectedly when she'd seen him before.

To her surprise and relief, it didn't come. Whatever had reminded her of Lucas, a trick of light and shadow, had vanished. The stranger in the back booth was just a skinny guy dressed in black pants and a curiously formal white shirt beneath an old tux jacket with the sleeves rolled up. Hunched over his cup of coffee, he could have been the model of a certain type of typical male Salem student who wanted to be an artist. Or a poet. Or at least look like one.

I'm getting twisted, she told herself. No way

that guy looks like Lucas at all. Talk about losing it!

As if he felt her scrutiny, the guy looked up. Janie realized that he was wearing dark glasses. She almost smiled. Dark glasses in a dimly lit coffee house in the darkest corner of the room.

Attitude, Janie thought. And good vision if he could see at all.

The dark glasses turned directly toward Janie. The smooth, predatory movement startled and unnerved her. She stared back, telling herself she was being childish.

That he was being childish. High-school punk. Rude. She felt as if she were being watched from behind a one-way mirror.

The customer isn't always right, she reminded herself, but the customer *is* always the customer. She turned abruptly away.

Crystal had come back from her tables and settled on one of the stools at the end of the counter. "Break time," she sang out.

With a quick survey of her two occupied tables, neither of whom seemed to need anything, Janie decided to take a break, too. She poured herself a cup of coffee and sat down at the counter next to Crystal, who'd already started nursing a cup of mocha java with whipped cream.

"Big plans for the weekend?" asked Crystal idly.

"I'm doing the Saturday night shift," said Janie.

"Gee, and I bet you've got some quality time planned for the library, too," said Crystal sarcastically. "I meant Salem U high society, hon. Boys. Dancing. Like that."

Janie shook her head.

"Shopping?" suggested Crystal.

"Nothing I need to buy," said Janie. "Sorry, Crys."

Crys took a noisy slurp of her mocha java. "He's not a bad tipper," she said.

"Who?"

"Mr. Mysterious over there. The guy dressed like the night stalker."

"Oh, *him*." Janie hesitated, then said, "You know, he doesn't remind me of Lu — of my ex at all. I don't know why I thought he did."

"You were thinking of him at the time," Crystal said wisely. "Your ex, I mean. Or he was thinking of you. Maybe that was it."

That's hardly possible, Janie thought. But before she could answer, Crystal said, "A lone ranger, female, coming in. Yours or mine?"

Turning to look at the girl who was coming in the door by herself, Janie laughed. "Mine. Definitely."

"You know her?" said Crystal.

"Forever. She's my roommate here . . ." Janie raised her arms and waved them at Susanne.

Her face brightening into a smile, Susanne hurried across the cafe.

"I can't believe I've never been here," she said. "It's so *cute*."

"I don't think that was what Norton had in mind," Crystal said. "Cute. I think he was going for, you know, sophisticated."

"Norton's the owner," explained Janie, seeing Susanne's confusion. "Susanne, this is Crystal, my fellow waitress. Crystal, this is Susanne, my roommate and best friend from childhood."

"Wow. One of those long relationships, huh?" Crystal smiled warmly at Susanne, but the smile Susanne gave Crystal back was merely polite.

Uh-oh, thought Janie, recognizing Susanne's immediate dislike of Crystal. I wonder what that's all about.

Susanne said to Janie, "It's half-time at the game and it's a great game and I think you should come see the end of it with me. I'm sitting there all by myself."

"You and a basketball stadium full of fans," said Janie, laughing. "And I know that you know some of the other girls who're dating the players."

"Tall, dark, and good hand skills?" asked Crystal. "I *do* like basketball players!"

Susanne gave Crystal another *small* smile.

"I think you should go, Janie," Crystal urged.

That got Susanne's attention. She looked directly at Crystal for the first time and appealed to her. "I do, too. Janie never enjoys herself. She works too hard, don't you think? I tried to get Janie to go with me tonight, but she said she had to work."

Rising to the bait, Crystal said immediately, "Had to work? Look at this place! It's dead."

"It won't be later," said Janie.

"Later, Will's coming in. He and I can handle anything, believe me. You're already working the Saturday night shift this weekend. You should go with Susanne, have some fun. Like I've been telling you."

"See?" said Susanne triumphantly.

Desperately, Janie said, "But I'm not dressed for it."

"Hey, these cafe uniforms can go *anywhere*." Crystal jumped off the stool and spun around. "The Morte par Chocolat dress code for waiters and waitresses: black pants or black jeans, white tailored shirt or sweater, black vest. Our tasteful attire makes us look like waitpersons, penguins — or girls dressed for a basketball game. Drop Morte Chic!"

"It's true," Susanne said, smiling more genuinely at Crystal while Janie groaned at Crystal's awful joke. "It's a cool uniform. It doesn't even look like one."

"Go on, Janine. Do it!" said Crystal. "Uh-oh. One of my tables is signaling."

Crystal left, wriggling her fingers at Susanne and Janie.

Janie sighed. "Don't you ever give up?"

"Never," said Susanne. "Are you coming?"

"Let me clear it with Norton."

Norton, as expected, merely said, "If it's okay with Crystal. Don't want her imposed on."

"She's already cleared me, Norton."

Norton smiled one of his slow, old-hippie smiles. "Far out," he said and turned back to the cake he was slicing.

As they walked out of the cafe, Crystal gave them a broad wink. Susanne pretended not to notice, but Janie couldn't help but smile.

It was only after she left that she realized she'd forgotten about the guy in the back booth. She shook her head, clearing the thought of him away. She hoped he gave Crystal a good tip.

The gym was rocking. Susanne led the way to their seats, excusing herself cheerfully to at least a dozen people, all of whom she knew by name.

"Poor lonely, friendless Susanne," teased Janie as they sat down.

"The third quarter just started!" a big, stocky guy whose build proclaimed him a football player roared in Janie's ear.

She nodded and smiled.

Susanne leaped to her feet, screaming wildly. Janie got up, too.

"Stretch, Stretch, Stretch!" Susanne screamed. Several people around them took up the chant. Janie got up to see what all the commotion was about, interested in spite of herself.

Out on the court, a boy who wasn't quite as tall as his Salem teammates did a half-backspin and shot up through a wall of opposing players to drop a perfect ball into the net.

The crowd went wild. "Isn't he fabulous?" Susanne shrieked in Janie's other ear.

"Fabulous," muttered Janie. They sat back down. "But I thought you were going out with Max."

"I am. But Max is sitting on the bench right now. And anyway, Max is good, but Stretch is *inspired*. You know?"

"Yes, but does Max?" cracked Janie.

Susanne gave Janie a playful whack on the arm. "Pay attention to the game. You'll have to talk about it at the party afterwards."

"Party? Who said anything about a party?"

But Susanne had leaped back up to cheer.

It was an exciting game. Even Janie had to admit that. She found herself pulled into the excitement, into the enthusiasm of the crowd. She hadn't been to a basketball game in a long time. She'd played on the girls' team in high school, but she hadn't been good enough to try out for the Salem women's team, even if she'd felt like it. Now it felt good to cheer, to be a part of the game again, even if it was only as a spectator. By the time the game had ended, she was jumping up just as quickly as Susanne and cheering just as loudly.

After the game, Susanne and Janie waited for the crowd to clear out as they sat in the bleachers. "It'll take 'em a little while to get the after-game speech from the coach and all," Susanne explained. "And I don't like hanging around the locker room door. Makes me feel like a groupie."

"So what do we do?"

"We make Max wait for *us*." Susanne grinned mischievously.

Sure enough, when Susanne finally decreed that it was time to leave the gym, they found Max lounging against the wall by the men's locker room entrance, talking to another guy not quite as tall as he was. Janie recognized him as Stretch.

Abandoning all pretense of indifference, Susanne hurled herself at Max. "Super fantastic game!" she cried. "You destroyed them!"

Max grinned and bent down to kiss her. Susanne's arms went up around his neck. For a moment, the two seemed oblivious to the onlookers.

Janie looked away. She'd run to Lucas like that, once. Now she never could again. Not in this lifetime . . .

"Hi. I'm David. Most folks call me Stretch, though."

Janie looked up. "Oh," she said, forcing herself back to the present. "Great game tonight."

To her surprise, Stretch actually ducked his head shyly. "Thanks," he said. He smiled at her. It was a nice smile. She found herself smiling back. Sandy brown hair, nice brown eyes, she noted. And a sweet expression that belied his fierceness on the basketball court.

"Ready to party?" Susanne's voice broke in on Janie's inventory.

Max, his arm around Susanne, added, "My car's waiting."

Shaking her head, Janie said, "No."

"Oh, Janie. Come on! We've got some celebrating to do!"

"Susanne, I'm glad you got me out of work to come to the game. It was a great game. You both played like maniacs, Max, Stretch . . . but I just don't feel like it."

"Come on, girl!" Max said.

Susanne drove her elbow into his ribs. It wasn't very subtle, but he got the hint.

"Of course, if you don't feel like it," Max added.

"Thanks. I'll make sure to catch the next game." Janie turned.

"We can give you a ride back to the dorm," Susanne said.

"I feel like walking," Janie said.

Unexpectedly, Stretch spoke. "I'll walk you back."

"But what about the party . . ." Max began. "Ow!" Susanne had clearly elbowed him a second time. "I mean, see you at the party, man."

"You don't have to do that," Janie said, looking up at Stretch.

"C'mon Max," Susanne said quickly and began dragging him away. "See you, Janie, Stretch!"

Janie watched them go, then looked back at Stretch. "Or maybe you do have to walk me back. Was Susanne trying to set you and me up?"

Stretch blushed again, but he grinned. "I dunno. She was pretty insistent about me coming with her and Max to the party. And she did ask me about a hundred times if I had a date."

"So how come you don't?" asked Janie, walking toward the gym exit. *Not that I really care,* she told herself.

Leaping ahead, Stretch held the door open for her. Janie walked out into the night hiding a smile. A polite, old-fashioned boy.

One her parents would probably love. But then, ever since what had happened to Lucas, her parents had been a lot more tolerant.

She wouldn't hold the fact that he was a nice guy that her parents would like against Stretch. "Thank you," she told him. "So, what do you do besides play basketball and not take dates to post-game parties?"

They shifted easily into conversation, walking the quiet, globelight-illuminated paths of Salem. Salem was an old school, with its share of ivy and gothic-looking buildings. A bell tower at the center of the campus marked the quarter hours with single, dolorous strokes and chimed the hours, a stroke for each hour that had passed. Sometimes Janie thought all Salem needed was a night watchman strolling the paths, calling out "One o'clock and all is well," just like in an old English play.

"I live in the Quad," she told Stretch as they crossed the heart of the campus.

"As long as I don't have to walk you back to Nightmare Hall," Stretch said.

"Nightmare Hall?" Janie shuddered. "Forget it." The shudder wasn't for effect. Ever since she'd heard the story of the poor girl who had died so tragically in brooding old Nightingale Hall, one of Salem's off-campus residences, she'd been haunted by it. Haunted too, by the thoughts of the people the girl had left behind. People who must have loved her. People who must ask themselves even now, over and over, *what could I have done to save her?*

Just as she had asked about Lucas. Over and over, thinking, if only I'd been earlier, I might have frightened the murderer away. Or seen who it was at least, been able to give some clue that might solve the crime.

But she'd been too late. She hadn't been able

to save Lucas. And she hadn't even been able to be a witness. Lucas's murderer still roamed free.

"Janie?"

"What? Oh! I'm sorry, Stretch. Nightmare Hall kind of gets to me . . . could we talk about something else?"

"I was," Stretch said. "I was talking about a date. You know, a real date."

Mortified, Janie impulsively put her hand on Stretch's arm. "I'm sorry!"

"Forgiveness is easy. Just go out with me." They stopped in front of the Quad. Stretch looked down at her and smiled his easy, bashful smile. His eyes crinkled at the corners, she noticed irrelevantly. He had one long, sandy brown lock of hair that kept falling forward, like a little kid's.

Janie didn't want to date, didn't want to go out with anyone ever again. No way would she ever risk being hurt a second time. No way would she ever chance the kind of loss she'd endured with Lucas.

She opened her mouth to say no and heard herself, looking up into Stretch's guileless brown eyes, say, "Yes, Stretch. I'd like that."

"You're forgiven," said Stretch, looking pleased. She thought for a moment he was going to punch her on the shoulder, just like a little boy who had a crush on a little girl in first grade. Instead he reached out and grabbed her hand and gave it a little squeeze. "I'll call you tomorrow. Right after lunch. Is that okay? I mean, it's not too early? And you don't have a class or anything, do you? Because if you do . . ."

"That's fine." She squeezed his hand back. "Talk to you tomorrow."

"Great!" Stretch strode off into the darkness.

Smiling to herself, Janie turned to go up the stairs into the entrance.

"Janie!"

She turned back. Stretch was standing at the corner. "See ya!" he called. He waved.

She waved back. "See you," she answered. She watched him stride away into the darkness.

For a long moment afterwards she stood, staring into the darkness, seeing nothing at all. That wasn't so bad, she was thinking. It was okay. Stretch was so easy, so normal. No hidden depths, no dark moods.

Lucas had wanted to be a writer. He brooded. He worried. He carried a notebook and took notes. It had all been very romantic and interesting.

But sometimes it had been . . .

No. She pushed the disloyal thought away. Stretch and Lucas were opposites. That was all. Opposite was good. Stretch would never, ever remind her of Lucas.

Lucas who was gone forever . . .

She turned again toward the door.

And it swooped down out of the sky. She felt it hiss through her hair. Instinctively she spun around. Something soft and warm and horrible caressed her face. She flung up her hands and felt the brush of fur. It blotted out the light. She turned desperately like a wild animal, and stumbled toward the stairs.

She fell.

She fought her way to her feet. If she could just reach the door.

The door. Oh, please, the door.

Her hand closed on the door handle.

It was on her again. Huge wings brushed her face. She yanked the door open. In the light from the entrance she saw a face pressing close to hers.

A mouth opened. A row of needle-sharp teeth . . .

It was an enormous bat.

"NOOOOOOOO!" she screamed.

Chapter 3

At the last minute it swerved and spun like a bit of charred black paper into the black sky.

She half fell through the door and into the lobby as the resident advisor on night desk duty came hurrying out.

"Are you okay?" she demanded, grabbing Janie's arm.

Janie got shakily to her feet. "I'm . . . it . . . it was a bat. A bat!"

"Come on inside. Did it bite you? Do you need to go to the infirmary?"

Mutely Janie shook her head. She took a deep breath. The RA guided her to a chair in the lobby and eased her down into it. "I'll get you a glass of water. Stay right there."

That was an order that was easy to obey. Janie leaned her head back and willed the trembling in her body to subside. It was just a bat, she told herself.

Just a bat. Ugh.

"Here." The RA had returned. She handed Janie a paper cup of water and Janie drank it down gratefully.

"Feel better?" the RA asked.

Janie nodded.

"It didn't bite you, did it? Because if it did, you have to go to the infirmary right away. Bats can carry rabies."

"No bites," Janie said.

"I wonder if it was rabid," the RA said, frowning. "Bats don't usually act that way. . . ."

"It didn't get me," Janie said firmly. She was beginning to recover her equilibrium. "Believe me, I'd know if it had."

She dunked the paper cup into a trash can near the chair and stood up. "Thank you."

The RA said, "Okay. If you're sure . . . you want me to call someone to walk you up to your room?"

"I'm fine. Really. Thanks again."

At last the RA nodded uncertainly and headed back to the front desk. Janie walked toward the door leading to the wing of the Quad where her room was. She forced herself to walk calmly, in case the RA was still watching. But inside, she was shaking. Her knees felt like jelly.

I hate bats, she thought.

"*Bats?*" Susanne said in disbelief, stopping in the act of yanking off her sweater. "You were attacked by *bats?*"

"*A* bat," said Janie. She hadn't been able to go to sleep. At last she'd just gotten out her probability and statistics book and started working equations, waiting for Susanne to come home.

Which took forever. Hey, Susanne, she'd thought, turning the page with a sigh, it's a school night.

But they weren't in high school anymore. They were adults now. They could do what they wanted, when they wanted, with whomever they wanted.

So she had only said, when Susanne finally came bounding in, "Some party, huh?"

Susanne had looked surprised, then pleased. "You went out with Stretch?" she had guessed. "You just got home."

"Nope . . ." Then Janie had told her about the bat.

"How big did you say it was?" Susanne said.

"Huge. Enormous." Janie held her hands apart.

"That's impossible," Susanne said. "Bats don't grow that big. Not even teenage mutant ninja bats . . ."

"Susanne, I'm serious. This gigantic bat came out of nowhere and tried to rip my eyes out. And, no, it didn't get me, so, no, I don't have to get tested for rabies."

"Good." Susanne got into her nightshirt and sat down at the foot of Janie's bed. "I'm not saying it didn't happen, Janie. It's just that bats really don't grow that big. *And* they don't attack people. They've got this incredible sonar. A bat can be flying at top speed and avoid a hair stretched across its path. I mean, it's awesome . . ."

"Susanne!"

"Sorry. You know I'm going to be a zoology major." Susanne looked sheepish. Then she said, thoughtfully, "I suppose if something was wrong with it, that might screw up its sonar and it might collide with you or something. And I know if a bat came out of nowhere and collided with me, I'd probably think it was elephant-sized.

"But you know what — it probably wasn't even a bat. It was probably somebody's pet myna bird or something. Or what about that professor who writes horror books? Doesn't she have a pet crow or something?"

Susanne seemed so matter-of-fact, so sure of herself, that Janie allowed herself to be persuaded. After all, Susanne should know. And both Susanne and the RA had said that it wasn't normal bat behavior.

It had been a long night. Maybe her imagination was making the incident into more than it was.

She looked up to find Susanne watching her intently.

Janie forced herself to smile. "Do I look like I've flipped out, as Norton would say? Don't worry. You're right. It was probably a pet bird or something . . . hey, guess what? Stretch said he was gonna call me tomorrow about a date."

Relaxing, Susanne smiled back, a huge, delighted smile. "He did. And you're gonna go, right? Tell me you said yes."

"I'm telling you."

"Great. That's great!" Susanne jumped up and headed for her own bed. "Now, get some beauty sleep, okay? In the morning we'll plan what you should wear on your first date with Stretch."

"Susanne, it's just a date."

Reaching up to turn out her light, Susanne

grinned wickedly. "You never know," she said. "You never know."

The knock on the door woke her. It was a sharp, authoritative rap, like an RA.

"It didn't bite me," Janie murmured sleepily. "It just tried to."

The knocking sounded again. In her bed across the room, Susanne slept heavily on.

Janie got up and stumbled to the door. "Shh," she said softly. "Just a minute."

The door opened. But the normally brightly lit hall of the Quad dorm was dark.

A shadowy figure stood in the doorway. A shadowy, familiar figure.

Janie felt her heart stop. "L-Lucas," she said in disbelief.

"Janie," he whispered. He held out his hand. "Invite me in."

"Oh, Lucas," she said, stepping back.

The light clicked on. "Janie?" said Susanne's voice. "Janie, what are you *doing*?"

Janie eyes met Lucas's. Suddenly she realized that it wasn't Lucas at all. Then he smiled. A thousand needle teeth flashed.

And Janie, staring up into the face of the bat, began to scream.

*　*　*

"Janie! Stop it! Stop it!"

Janie opened her eyes. She was standing at the door of her room. Susanne was beside her, shaking her shoulder.

"Lucas," Janie whimpered, before she could stop herself.

"You had a nightmare," Susanne said. "You were sleepwalking."

Shakily Janie raised her hand to her forehead. It was beaded with sweat.

"Nightmare," she repeated. "Right. Oh my God, it was awful."

"It was just a dream. Come back to bed."

For the second time that night, Janie allowed herself to be mutely led somewhere, this time to her bed.

"Go to sleep," Susanne ordered. "And don't have any more nightmares."

"Okay," said Janie. She heard her voice, small and scared as a child. She cleared her throat. "Okay," she said again. There, that sounded better.

Susanne said, "I'm going to leave my light on for a little while."

"Thanks, Susanne," said Janie with real gratitude. She let her head drop down on her pillow.

And fell instantly into a deep and dreamless sleep.

Striding across campus the next day, Janie thought, I've got bats in the belfry, that's what. It was hard to believe that she'd ever had an encounter with a bat the night before. And the shadow of the nightmare, the thing with Lucas's form and a bat's face, was also receding under the bright light of a clear and beautiful day.

Janie checked her mail, checked her watch, and did double time up the steps and toward Griswold Hall, where Susanne was completing her zoology lab. Janie had talked to Stretch, agreed to go out with him on Friday night, and then knocked off all her homework. Now she wanted to tell Susanne about the upcoming date.

She felt good. *Maybe all it takes is a bat and a nightmare*, she thought.

The last classes of the day were just letting out. The sun was setting and the evening shadows beginning to lengthen. Janie sat down on the stone railing at the edge of the steps leading up to the building to wait for Susanne.

But when Susanne came out, Janie barely even saw her.

Because she couldn't keep her eyes off the

gorgeous guy that Susanne was talking to.

Gorgeous. It wasn't a word Janie had ever used for a guy. Or ever meant to.

But it was true. He was gorgeous. Intensely, amazingly, otherworldly gorgeous. In the early twilight, he practically glowed.

"Susanne!" Janie said, glad she'd worn her oldest, tightest jeans, glad she'd taken the time to fluff her honey-red hair around her face instead of leaving it pulled back in the austere waitress bun she usually wore.

Susanne stopped. A shadow crossed her face. Or had Janie imagined Susanne's look of displeasure?

Then Susanne was smiling a normal Susanne smile. "Janie," she said. She hurried toward Janie. "See ya," she said over her shoulder to the gorgeous guy.

But he kept up with Susanne and stopped at her elbow when she reached Janie. "Hi, there," he said, looking directly into Janie's eyes.

"Hello," she said, unable to look away. Were eyes that color of blue legal? And since it was clear that Susanne wasn't going to introduce them to each other, she added, "I'm Janie."

"Bram," he said.

"We have to go," said Susanne. She grabbed Janie's arm and practically dragged her away.

"See you," she repeated as they left.

"See *you*," said Bram. He sounded as if he was laughing. But when Janie looked back, he was standing, motionless and unsmiling, right in the middle of the walk where they had left him.

Staring at her.

"Weren't you kind of rude?" asked Janie, rubbing her arm.

Susanne kept walking. Then she said, "I'll admit he's sexy, okay. He's the nicest thing that ever happened to female eyesight on this campus, okay. But he knows it, Janie. You don't want anything to do with him, trust me."

Nettled, Janie said, "I think I can take care of myself, Susanne."

"Can you?" Susanne stopped. She faced Janie. "Can you?"

"Geez, can't I just admire the way a guy looks? I didn't say I wanted to marry him. Chill out."

When Susanne didn't lose her serious look, Janie said, "Besides, I just accepted a date on Friday night with Stretch. That's what I came to tell you."

The ploy worked again as it had the night before. The troubled look left Susanne's face to be replaced by one of simple delight. "Excellent," she said. "This is truly excellent. What's the plan?"

Relieved that Susanne was no longer fixing her with one of her world-class brooding looks, Janie told her about the conversation with Stretch. But she couldn't banish the image of Bram from her mind. She knew that Stretch or no Stretch — and Lucas or no Lucas — she had to see Bram again.

Chapter 4

"Hey Norton, say it's closing time," Crystal said that evening, as she and Janie sat at the counter at Morte par Chocolat.

Norton grinned. "Saying something doesn't make it so."

"It does if *you* say it, Norton. Puh-leasssse?"

"Get out of here," said Norton. "I can shut down the shop. Be sure and flip the closed sign over on your way out the door."

"All right!" Crystal whirled around and seized Janie by the sleeve. "Didja hear that, Janester?"

"I heard," Janie lowered her voice. "But we've still got a customer."

Crystal looked over Janie's shoulder and a funny look came over her face. "Yeah," she said flatly. "Well, leave him to Norton, too."

The mysterious guy — the one whom Janie had thought looked like Lucas that first night

— was back again, lodged in the back corner booth. He'd come in late that night. He'd been sitting, a cup of coffee growing cold between his hands, ever since.

"Maybe you could ask him to your party," said Janie, dropping her order pad in the waitress drawer.

"He's starting to give me the creeps," said Crystal. "Besides, *you're* the one coming to the party."

"What is this, a conspiracy? I was out late last night, thanks to Susanne and you. Now you want to keep me out late tonight?" Janie shook her head, "Thanks, but no thanks."

"Yes, thanks," Crystal insisted. "What do you think, that I'd take you to some typical Salem U frat-rat blowout? I don't think so. Girl, you are coming with me. Off campus. *Way* off campus."

From behind the order window Norton said, "Beat it, you two."

"See?" said Crystal. Before Janie could argue anymore, she found herself being steered out the door. Crystal stopped at the door and flipped the open sign over so that it said closed.

And stopped. "Geez," she said.

"Wha — " Janie stopped too.

The mysterious stranger was standing up,

uncoiling, almost. He looked like a long, black, mean slash across the funky decor of Morte par Chocolat. One long slender hand went into the pocket of the jacket he was wearing and bills floated to the table. He turned. The twin black shields of his sunglasses seemed to flash in the gloom.

"He's headed this way," whispered Crystal with only half-exaggerated nervousness. "Let's get outta here."

Janie didn't argue. And she didn't look back.

"Who *is* that guy?" she gasped as they fell into Crystal's beat-up old car.

"A creep," said Crystal decisively.

"Why does he keep hanging around? Where does he come from?"

"I don't know. And I'm not going to get close enough to ask." Crystal gunned the motor and they roared out of the parking lot and into the night.

The party was pumping. Nor had Crystal been lying. It was definitely no Salem frat-rat bash, although when they reached the vast, rambling old house on the edge of town, Janie recognized a few faces from campus.

But other faces were unfamiliar. Many were

older. Wearier. More worldly and sophisticated.

Crystal stopped in the doorway, put her hands on her hips and surveyed the room with frank appraisal. Almost immediately a body danced out of the crowd. "You twins?" he asked.

"Identical," said Crystal, sizing him up in a glance. "Come on, sis," she said to Janie and led her quickly away. "We can do better than that," she explained as they came up beside the refreshment table.

"I like the look," said a familiar voice. "The pulled-back hair, the nun-like quality of the black and white. It has an austere quality that suits you."

Slowly, feeling the smile inside that she was determined to be too cool to show on the outside, Janie turned. "Hello," she said. "I see you haven't changed since we met."

It was true. Bram was still wearing the same black jeans and white T-shirt he'd been wearing that afternoon.

But as he immediately pointed out, pretending to look hurt, "This time I have a leather jacket on."

"And a nice one, too," Crystal said. "I'm Crystal. Janie and I work together."

"Hi," said Bram. His blue eyes were phenomenal even in the dim light of the party, and they had their effect. Crystal's mouth dropped slightly open.

"Can I get you two a drink?" offered Bram. A moment later he was threading his way back through the crowd, and Crystal had Janie's arm in a death grip.

"I can't believe you never told me about him!" Crystal hissed.

"Hey, I just met him myself today."

"You're kidding. The way he was looking at you. I thought . . ." Crystal stopped and sighed. "Listen to what I just said. He was looking at *you*, not me. Some girls have all the luck."

"Crys!"

Bram returned and held out their drinks.

"Thanks," said Crystal brightly. She fixed Bram with her most melting look and said, "Well, I see someone I have to say hello to. Later, you guys."

"Crystal!" Janie said again, exasperated. But not too exasperated. Bram's nearness was having an effect on her. An effect she'd almost forgotten.

She glanced up at him through her lashes to find him watching her. Catching her eye, he smiled.

It was a confident smile, full of promise.

"Well?" said Janie, challengingly. She reminded herself of Susanne's words. Bram was bad news. Gorgeous and he knew it. Used to an easy victory. Used to having girls fall all over him.

But not her.

He lifted his eyebrows. "Let's dance," he said, and without waiting for her answer pulled her out onto the twisting, pulsing heat of the dance floor and close against his body.

What seemed like hours later, Janie saw the glint of Crystal's silvery hair beside her. She smiled. Crystal looked like she was having fun.

Almost as much fun as Janie. If fun was what you called it, this heart-pounding sensation, this feeling of nerves and anticipation.

This feeling of being alive again.

Bram had danced her to the edge of the floor.

"Another drink," he said. "Or a ride home?"

"A ride home," said Janie. She paused then said, "I live on campus."

If he'd been suggesting taking her to his place, he never showed it. "Yeah," he said. "I know my way around. I lived on campus once, too."

Bram caught her hand and turned to go. Across the room, Janie caught Crystal's eye and pointed at Bram. Crystal nodded, making her eyes round and amazed.

They didn't talk much as they walked out of the party, down the line of cars on either side of the road.

"Where's your car?" asked Janie at last.

"Here." Bram stopped.

Janie looked around. Then she said, "That?" She pointed at a gleaming Harley Davidson motorcycle parked at the side of the road.

"That," said Bram. "Still want that ride?"

"You have an extra helmet?"

"I come prepared," said Bram. Sure enough, two helmets were locked to the back of the bike.

More amused than annoyed by Bram's ego, and his assumption that of course he'd be taking a girl home from the party, Janie said, "So which helmet is mine?"

Bram grinned and bent over to unlock the helmets and the bike. A few minutes later, they were roaring into the darkness, Janie pressed close against the back of Bram's leather jacket. The dark streets flashed by, then the lights of Salem, strobing like the lights of the party. Then they were shooting through the massive stone gates at the entrance to the campus. Bram, Janie noted, knew the way to the Quad without having to ask.

He pulled to a stop at the curb in front of

Quad Main. It was quite a different arrival than the one with Stretch the night before. People noticed Bram and not only because of the distinctive guttural noise of the Harley. He was dramatic, bold.

Exciting.

Two girls going in the door of the Quad turned to stare. Janie was sure that others were at their windows facing out onto the street, staring down at them.

As she took off her own helmet, Bram pulled his helmet off to rest it on the bike in front of him and said over his shoulder, "I bet you've never had a ride like that before."

"Not on a Harley, no," Janie said coolly. She got off and locked her helmet in its place on the back seat bar of the bike.

Bram laughed. He reached out and caught Janie's wrist. He pulled her slowly forward. She leaned back against his pull just a little, teasing, smiling into his eyes.

Then his arm was around her and he was kissing her. Not a friendly, polite getting-to-know-you kiss like Stretch would have given her. It was deep and passionate and demanding.

And it shook Janie to the core. She pulled back quickly, feeling her cheeks burn at the look in Bram's eyes.

"Where and when?" he asked softly, self-assured laughter in his voice.

"Call me," Janie said. She stepped back. "Maybe I'll let you take me for another ride."

Bram smiled a slow smile and nodded. Then he put his helmet back on, kicked the bike into gear and gunned away into the darkness.

The harsh rumble of the motor faded into the night.

It was replaced by another sound. A sound that sent cold chills up Janie's spine. A single keening note, mocking and mournful at the same time.

It was a sound she knew she'd never heard before. And yet it was so familiar. So terrifyingly familiar. As if someone — or something — was calling her name in a special secret language.

But it wasn't that at all.

Even as she placed it, even as she realized what it was — and what it could not be — the howl of the wolf died away.

"Did Stretch meet you after work?" Susanne asked.

"What are you doing up so late?" asked Janie.

"Don't tell anyone — studying — so did he?"

"Was he supposed to?" Janie countered. "I

thought he and I had a date for *tomorrow* night."

With an exasperated sigh, Susanne said, "You *do*. But he said something to Max about meeting you after work."

"Well, he wasn't there when I got off," Janie answered evasively. For some reason, Susanne's questions annoyed her. She was beginning to feel stifled by Susanne's attention — and although she liked Stretch, she didn't like Susanne's automatic assumption that she and Stretch were made for each other.

Fortunately, Susanne didn't notice Janie's evasiveness — or realize that the cafe had long since closed. She was too focused on her matchmaking schemes. "Too bad," she said.

Janie forced herself to smile. "Maybe he'll have better luck tomorrow," she said lightly. She grabbed her bathrobe. "I'm gonna hit the shower. See you in a few."

Susanne had already left for class the next morning when Janie got up, a fact for which she was profoundly grateful. She dawdled over getting ready in her room, enjoying having it all to herself, away from Susanne's questions and observant eyes.

She'd slept well the night before and she felt

more buoyant and alive then she had felt in months. One class, she thought, and it's art history, which is fun. I can rattle off my homework in the library this afternoon. And hang out a little at the Student Center before I come back to the dorm to get ready for my date with Stretch.

Hanging out, she realized, meant sitting in a conspicuous place on the terrace of the Student Center — just in case Bram happened to stroll by.

Pushing the nagging feeling of disloyalty to Lucas aside, she spent extra care on choosing her outfit for the day, settling at last on the worn, skin-tight jeans she'd first been wearing when she'd met Bram, black boots that she decided looked vaguely motorcyclish, and a loose off-the-shoulder sweater over a stretch-lace chemise. Not her usual look, but she liked it.

She thought Bram might, too . . . if she happened to run into him.

Just one kiss, she thought in wry amusement. That's all it took. One kiss.

One very different kiss.

Smiling, she bounded out of the dorm and into her perfect day.

* * *

"We come last," the professor said, "to a painting with which I am sure many of you are familiar . . ."

Janie studied the painting and wrote down the notes. She laughed dutifully at the professor's parting joke and made a big circle and a star in her notebook around the date of an upcoming test in the class. As class ended, she bent over, reached under her seat, and dragged her green backpack out. She unzipped the top and shoved the notebook inside. Then she fished around and pulled out her date book to record the test date in it as well. Her date book was her life, as she had once told Susanne only half-jokingly. In it was her class schedule, her work schedule, her study schedule, and a hundred reminders of all the things she needed to do to keep all the bits and pieces of her overbooked life running smoothly.

She propped the heavy black date book on her knee and flipped it open ahead to the test week.

And stopped. A heavy, cream-colored piece of paper folded neatly in half had been inserted in the pages.

Janie frowned. Had she scribbled some note to herself and forgotten it? Talk about having too much to do!

Without any premonition of danger, she unfolded the heavy paper.

Her eyes widened. She took a sharp breath — and forgot to breathe again.

"No," she whispered. "It's impossible. It can't be."

But it was.

In Lucas's familiar handwriting, in slashing black across the page, screamed the words:

Sweet Jane: Love You Forever.

The paper burned her fingers. The words burned her eyes.

Sweet Jane.

Lucas's name for her. His private, special name for her, whispered in her ear in the dark between kisses.

Love you forever, Sweet Jane. Love you forever . . .

With a cry, Janie crumpled the note into a ball and thrust it into the bottom of her pack. It wasn't possible.

Who would do such a cruel and terrible thing? Who could possibly know what Lucas had called her, that special, private name?

It was a horrible, evil joke. The product of a sick, sick mind.

Looking wildly around, Janie realized that

the classroom was empty. She jumped up so suddenly that the desk fell over with a clatter, but she didn't stop to fix it. She fled from the room as if all the dark forces of the earth were at her heels.

She didn't go hang out after all. She went to the library. Claimed a desk in a quiet corner but not out of sight of the other students who chose to study rather than play on a beautiful, spring-like Friday afternoon. Janie sat there with her books open in front of her. She did some work, mechanically. Later, as she handed in assignments, she wouldn't remember completing them or even what they were about.

Because mostly, through the long afternoon, turning the pages aimlessly, listening to the muffled gong of the clock chiming the quarter hours in the clock tower, she thought of the note buried in the bottom of her pack.

Sweet Jane Forever.

No one had ever known those words. She'd never told a soul, not even Susanne. She'd remembered them bitterly, silently, standing dry-eyed beside Lucas's grave.

Sweet Jane Forever, she'd said to him silently. But you lied to me, Lucas. You told me forever and you swore you'd never lie.

That makes two lies you told me.

And then a thought as cold and frightening

as death came: suddenly she saw Lucas lying on the ground as she had found him. Saw herself kneeling frantically above him, pleading with him to live.

To not be dead.

And heard the frantic mantra that she had chanted, for that one awful, eternal moment before reality and realization had set in.

"Lucas," she'd murmured, into his deaf ears, "Lucas, it's me. Sweet Jane. Sweet Jane Forever, Lucas, remember? Lucas? Forever. You promised. I love you forever. Lucas, don't leave me . . ."

Had the killer still been there? Had Lucas's murderer heard her frantic words?

Had he come back for her?

"Janie?"

She must have jumped a mile.

"Sorry. I didn't mean to startle you." Stretch's kind, earnest face swam into her line of sight and Janie returned to the moment with something like relief.

It's Friday night, she told herself. I have a date, a real date with a nice guy. I'm safe with him. I'm going to enjoy myself.

Sweet Jane Forever.

I won't think about it. Stretch won't let anything happen to me.

She reached out her hand and slid it into Stretch's. "Hi," she said. "I'm glad to see you," she said, and she meant it.

More than he would ever know.

They went to the movies. An easy, simple date. Even the movie was easy, a comedy where no one died and the ending was sure to be a happy one. It was the first movie Janie had been to since Lucas had been murdered. She thought that seeing such a silly movie would annoy her.

She didn't think she'd be able to laugh.

But she found herself laughing and sharing popcorn with Stretch. And when Stretch suggested, nervously, that they go for a drive in the country, she agreed.

"There's an overlook out at Bottomless Lake," said Stretch, referring to a nearby state park. "We could go, uh, take in the view."

"Why not?" she said, liking Stretch for his nervousness, for his predictability. It was so old-fashioned, in a way. A date, a drive to a local parking spot. She smiled at Stretch. "I've never been there before."

"You haven't? Great!"

It soon became apparent, as they drove down the dark lanes leading to Bottomless Lake, that Stretch had never been there either. He had to stop several times to consult the signs marking the way to the overlook.

At last they pulled to a stop in a small parking area. Stretch turned off the motor and cleared his throat. He jumped out of the car and ran around to the other side and opened the door for her.

When Janie was out, he cleared his throat again and said, "I think the view is over there." Janie let him take her hand and lead her to the railing along the overlook.

"Not bad," she said softly. Above them, a half moon surrounded by stars lit the clear dark sky. Across the lake, the tops of trees made a jagged horizon. Below, the still, inky waters reflected the moon and the stars.

The night was profoundly still. Not even a breeze touched the trees. They might have been in a painting, or a photograph. For a moment Janie felt uneasy. As if she were being watched. As if she were caught inside the frame of that painting or photograph and someone was on the outside watching her. Someone evil. A tremor of fear shook her as she remembered the note. *Sweet Jane Forever.*

Had the murderer put it there? Had he followed her to Salem? Had he followed her here?

Stretch leaned down to kiss her.

It was a schoolboy kiss, tentative, gentle, sweet.

Careful.

Nice.

Not like Bram's. Not like Lucas's. It didn't make the world go away. And yet . . .

Stretch's arms tightened. Janie leaned toward him, willing him to make her forget her fear, her past. Herself.

Then, abruptly, he let her go. He stepped slightly back and stared down at her, still holding her in the loose circle of his arms.

"Janie, I think there's something you ought to know," he began.

But before he could go on, Janie stiffened in his arms. "Stretch! No! Look out! LOOOK OUT!"

Chapter 5

With all her might, Janie pulled Stretch to one side and down.

Even as she fell, she hoped it was a bad dream. Even as she fell, she knew it was real.

The wolf hurtled toward them, its enormous shape blotting out the night, its eyes gleaming yellow in the blackness of its form.

It was huge. And horrifyingly silent. Janie saw it rise up above them. She saw the flash of wickedly curving fangs.

"No!" she screamed.

For a moment the lethal shape seemed to hover uncertainly in the air. Then she saw it land without breaking stride, saw it melt away into the shadows. In all the stillness that surrounded them, it never made a sound.

"Uh, Janie?"

Janie realized that Stretch was lying on top of her. Embarrassed, she pushed him away and scrambled to her feet. She swung around to face in the direction in which the wolf had disappeared.

"Did you see it?" she panted.

Stretch came to stand beside her. He put his arm tentatively around her shoulder. "See what?"

"The wolf!" Janie screamed. "The *wolf*! It *attacked* us!"

"I didn't see anything," said Stretch calmly.

"It was a huge, enormous wolf. It came from that way!" Janie pointed wildly, her hand shaking. Although it was a cool night, she realized she was sweating. The sweat of fear.

"Janie, that way is the lookout. Whatever it was that you think you saw . . ."

"I did see it!"

". . . okay, but whatever it was couldn't have come from that direction. It would have had to come straight up the side of a cliff."

"I know what I saw." Janie clenched her teeth and forced herself to speak slowly and clearly. "There's enough light up here to see clearly and I saw it. It had yellow eyes and it was huge."

"A wild dog, maybe," said Stretch, sliding his hand under her elbow and beginning to walk her back to the car.

"No!" said Janie. It couldn't have been. She

knew that. She didn't know how she knew, but she did.

Stretch opened the car door and she found herself climbing inside. How could Stretch be so calm, so unafraid? How could he not have seen the wolf? Or sensed its presence?

Starting the car up, Stretch steered it carefully out of the parking area and back through the dark, deserted roads. Janie let her eyes turn toward the shifting shapes of woods and fields that they passed. She was looking for the wolf.

She knew it was still there. She knew it was still with them, racing along beside the car, unseen . . .

She knew it. The hound of hell.

With a cough, Stretch cleared his throat. Then he said, "Are you okay?"

Something about the way he said it caught Janie's attention. "I'm fine," she said. "As good as any girl who's had a wolf two inches from her head can be."

"I've never been called a wolf before," Stretch joked feebly, reaching out to put his hand over Janie's.

"You don't believe me, do you?" Janie said. And then she knew. With a sudden flash of fury, she knew. "Of course you don't," she went on. "Because Susanne's had a little talk with you, hasn't she? Told you I'm not myself. That I've gone a little crazy. So of course it follows that I'm imagining things."

"Janie."

"It's true. Tell me!" Janie jerked her hand away from his.

Putting his hand back on the steering wheel, Stretch stared straight ahead.

"Tell me!"

"Okay. But it's not what you think. Susanne just said, you know, that you'd, that your boyfriend had been killed. That you were still shaken up about it. That you might not be ready for . . ."

"Oh, *great*! Why didn't she just take out an advertisement in the newspaper? Or put up signs around campus? After all, what right do I have to privacy?"

"She was just trying to . . ."

"I know what she was trying to do. Interfere. It's a problem Susanne has. A big problem."

"Janie."

Knowing she was being childish, Janie folded her arms and stared stonily ahead. When they reached the dorm, Stretch said, "I'll call you."

"Good night," said Janie. She counted it a victory that she didn't slam the door.

Susanne wasn't home. She was on a date

with Max, of course. She wouldn't be home for a long, long time.

Maybe it was just as well, Janie thought grimly before she fell into sleep. Because when I get my hands on her, *I just might kill her.*

Still fuming when she awoke the next morning, Janie dressed quickly and quietly and left before her roommate woke up. She spent the day studying and went to the cafe early, before her shift had started.

Will, who was doing the end of the shift all alone, slid a cup of coffee along the counter to her and went back to the chem book he had open in front of him. Janie propped her hand on her chin and stared at nothing.

Until *he* sat down beside her.

"Hi," he said.

He had a low, flat, uninflected voice, like a newscaster who wasn't particularly interested in the news. Janie turned slowly toward the mysterious stranger.

He was dressed just like always, dark pants, a white shirt buttoned up to the throat, an old tux jacket with satin lapels, the sleeves rolled up. He wore soft, expensive-looking black leather shoes on his feet.

His glasses were black mirrors. She could

see herself in them. They made his skin seem ghostly.

"Hello," she said.

He flicked a finger in Will's direction to indicate that he'd have a coffee too. His movements were quick and graceful. "Jon," he said.

"Janie," she replied reluctantly.

He nodded. Will appeared with a cup of coffee.

"You come here a lot," she noted. "Will knew how you wanted your coffee without asking."

He didn't answer. He kept the glasses focused on her face.

Suddenly exasperated, she said, "It's rude to stare, okay?"

He leaned back a little at that. But he didn't take off his glasses. A slight smile flickered at the corner of his mouth. "I didn't mean to stare. But you remind me of someone."

Forgetting her dislike of him, Janie said, "Really? Because that's just what I thought when I first saw you in here."

"We have so much in common," he said. It sounded like he was being sarcastic. Sort of.

Janie replied stiffly, "It was only for a moment. The moment passed."

"Time flies when you're having fun."

That did it. Janie pushed her coffee cup back

and said, "I start my shift soon. I'd better go put my gear away."

"Maybe I could walk you home afterwards," he said.

"No. Thanks. Someone is meeting me," she lied hastily.

Although she knew it was impossible, she thought something flashed behind the sunglasses. But all Jon said was, "Another time maybe."

"Maybe," she said. *In your dreams*, she added to herself.

He was gone when she came back out. Crystal was just arriving.

"Did you see him?" she asked Crystal.

"Who?" Crystal sounded out of breath.

"The mystery guy. His name is Jon. He sat down next to me at the counter."

Crystal looked around the restaurant. She lowered her voice. "You know who he reminds me of?"

"One of your ex guys?"

Her eyes huge, Crystal shook her head vigorously. "I'm serious. He reminds me of that vampire guy in the movie."

"Dracula? Jon the good tipper with attitude reminds you of *Dracula*?"

"Laugh if you want," Crystal said with dignity. "But I mean it. He gives me the creeps.

Strange things have happened on this campus before, you know. A vampire wouldn't surprise me at all."

Janie opened her mouth to make another crack, then stopped abruptly. She remembered the bat that had swooped down on her.

The long, drawn-out, unearthly howl of the wolf. The deadly silence as it had leaped past her on the overlook.

A cold chill crept up her spine.

Strange things have happened on this campus before.

She turned away and walked toward her first customer of the evening without answering.

Janie half-expected him to come back right before the restaurant closed. She made Crystal promise to stay and walk out with her.

"Not that I believe in vampires," she told Crystal, "so don't look so smug. But he *is* strange."

"Have you ever seen him by the light of day?" asked Crystal. "Vampires don't go out in the daylight."

"Lots of people who hang out at this cafe don't go out by the light of day, Crystal." Janie hoisted her pack to her shoulder, waved goodbye to Norton, and headed out the door with Crystal beside her.

"More than one party is happening out there tonight," Crystal said persuasively.

Janie shook her head. "I've had enough socializing for one week," she answered. *More than enough*, she thought wryly, thinking of Bram and of Stretch and of all the weird things that had happened.

Sweet Jane Forever.

She pushed that thought from her mind.

They crossed Pennsylvania Avenue onto the campus.

Janie stopped. "Did you . . ."

"What?"

"I don't know." Janie gave a little laugh. "I don't know. For a moment I had the strangest feeling that we were being followed."

"Jon!" said Crystal immediately, swinging around.

In spite of herself, Janie found she was following Crystal's example, turning in a slow circle to survey the surrounding campus.

But no one was there, except distant couples walking beneath the globe lamps that lined the walkways beneath the ancient oak trees.

"C'mon," said Janie. "We're being silly."

"Next time, I'm wearing a garlic necklace," said Crystal.

"Do you think dabbing garlic juice behind your ears would work?" Janie asked.

The thought made them both giggle.

"You know, if there were vampires, and all that stuff really worked, vampires would have been gone long time ago," said Janie.

"Maybe that's why there are still vampires," argued Crystal. "Because no one believes in them, so they don't do all that stuff, like wear garlic necklaces and crosses of silver and all."

"I wonder what other stuff there is that stops them?" Janie said. "Or what makes a vampire."

Crystal shuddered. "I don't want to know." She stopped at the corner. "Your dorm is just a couple of blocks away. Can you make it, or will the vampires get you?"

"I'll make it, but what about you?" Janie kept her voice light, but she couldn't shake the feeling of uneasiness that suddenly swept over her.

Crystal apparently didn't share it. She laughed. "It's early. And we just passed a campus cop. See ya." With a wave of her hand, she was gone, heading across campus and out toward her apartment.

Feeling unsettled and slightly melodramatic and foolish, Janie began to walk toward the dorm.

Silence fell. Thick, unnatural silence. Suddenly nothing moved. Nothing breathed.

All life waited . . .

Waited . . .

Janie stopped. As if in slow motion she turned her head.

The wolf stood in the shadows. It was enormous, even bigger than she remembered. Its eyes gleamed yellow in the darkness.

"Go away!" Janie croaked.

At the sound of her voice, the wolf's eyes suddenly blazed from golden yellow to hellfire red.

She tried to scream. But she couldn't make a sound. Janie began to run.

And the wolf ran, too.

Chapter 6

She was going to die. It was going to kill her.

Her heart slammed against her chest. Her breath strangled her.

She ran on. The dorm seemed to be miles away. A lifetime away.

It ran beside her. Pacing her. Toying with her.

A figure emerged on the corner ahead. With a last desperate burst of strength, Janie ran toward it.

A campus cop. He spun at the sound of her pounding footsteps. Caught her arm as she nearly fell over.

"Whoa, what is it?" He peered past her, looking, searching.

But he didn't see it. Janie could tell. His questioning eyes came back to her face as she tried to catch her breath.

"Wolf . . . chased me," she panted. "It . . . I . . ."

"I've told them about keeping him fenced or on a leash!" The cop sounded more annoyed than concerned.

Janie was so surprised that her mouth dropped open.

"I'll go over there right now and give the fraternity officers a good talking to. But you needn't worry, young lady. He's friendly. Just a big puppy still, needs to learn some manners."

"Puppy?" How much bigger could a wolf get? Was she going crazy?

"The German shepherd the frat boys have. It's the frat house mascot. Great dog. They rescued it from a shelter . . ." As Stretch had done the night before, the cop was steering her along. Before she knew it, she was standing outside the Quad.

"It wasn't a dog," she said desperately. "It was a wolf."

"No wolves in these parts," said the cop. "But I'll take care of it, don't you worry." He patted her shoulder and opened the door of the dorm. Speechless, shocked, Janie stepped inside and watched as he walked briskly back into the night.

"It wasn't a dog," she whispered. "It wasn't."

"It wasn't a wolf," said Susanne firmly. Forgetting her anger at Susanne in her terror over what had just happened, Janie had poured out the whole story. Although she suspected, from Susanne's expressionless demeanor, that Stretch had already told her the part about the wolf the night before.

"It was. It was!"

Susanne said, "It couldn't have been. There are no wolves around here. And even if there were, a wolf wouldn't act like that. They avoid humans, they don't eat them. In fact, their primary source of food is small animals, like mice . . ."

"I'm not a mouse!" Janie heard her voice shaking. She swallowed hard. "It was . . ."

"A wild dog, probably. Now that's something to be scared of. They aren't naturally afraid of people the way wolves are. And some of those mixed breeds get to be pretty gigantic."

Janie said, "You really believe that's what it was?"

"I do," said Susanne firmly.

She sounded so sure. Just as the cop had. Just as Stretch had.

Maybe they were right. Maybe it was a huge, wild dog. Or maybe it was even that fraternity's mascot, escaped from the frat house.

She was letting things get to her. And she couldn't do that. She had to stay strong. Because if she didn't, if she started to remember what had happened to Lucas, if she started to cry, she might never stop.

"Okay," she said at last. She met Susanne's eyes and hoped she looked reassured. Sane.

She wondered how many other people Susanne had told about what had happened to Lucas. She wondered how many people knew her tragic secret. Did they point? Did they whisper? Would Susanne go around and tell them that poor Janie was imagining things now? That poor Janie was fragile and had to be treated gently, carefully?

Had she told Stretch that? Would Stretch tell other people . . .

Sweet Jane Forever.

Had Susanne sent that note?

Susanne and Lucas had been friends. Had they been more than friends? Had they been secret lovers? Was that how Susanne knew?

Maybe Susanne blamed Janie for Lucas's death . . .

No. No, that was crazy. She was going

crazy. She had to stop thinking like this. Wolves. Bats. Vampires.

It wasn't possible.

"I need some rest," she said slowly. "I'm going to bed."

"Good idea," said Susanne heartily. She sounded like a doctor talking to a sick but stubborn patient.

At that moment, Janie hated her best friend. Hated her more than she'd ever hated anyone except whoever murdered Lucas.

And she'd never felt more alone in her life.

The Quad caf, Janie saw with relief, was almost empty. She grabbed a cup of coffee and a table by the window and sat staring out at nothing and yawning. It was too early to be up. But she had awakened long before her alarm had gone off for her first class, and she hadn't been able to get back to sleep.

A few other students were trickling in to the caf, the all-nighter crowd, mostly. They'd spent the night in their rooms, if their roommates were tolerant, or in one of the many rooms that were in the basement that ran beneath the Quad, studying for some test or other. They'd come to the Quad caf, which had even worse coffee than the main dining hall over in the Student Center, because they weren't quite ready to admit defeat. They were still in their rumpled clothes from the day before. They still clutched notebooks and books with thousands of bookmarks and pencils, as if another hour of studying were going to make a difference.

But then, who knew? Janie thought. Maybe it would, with the help of a little coffee. She'd never had to pull an all-nighter yet for school. The only thing that kept her up all night was bad dreams.

She got up to get more coffee and snagged a bagel. Heading back to her table, she saw an abandoned newspaper on an empty table.

Maybe, she thought wryly, she'd find something in one of the advice columns that would solve her life: *Dear Abby, I'm being pursued by bats and wolves. I haven't told my flaky friend yet because she'd just say it was all part of the plot of the local vampire to take over the world; I did tell my best friend and she thinks I'm the flake.*

She took a sip of coffee and stared down at the cup in surprise. The coffee actually tasted decent for once.

Maybe I really am sick, she thought. She smiled and flipped the paper over.

The smile froze on her face.

CAMPUS COP KILLED the headline said.

Beneath it were two pictures: a head shot of the campus security guy she'd talked to the night before. To the right of that, a fuzzy shot of a covered body.

In disbelief she read, hardly comprehending the words. Sometime shortly after midnight, he'd been found, apparently stabbed through the throat twice with a sharp slender object. Salem town police had no suspects.

"I thought I'd find you here!"

Janie looked up. It was Susanne, dressed and carrying her backpack. "I'm getting an early start on class today," Susanne explained brightly.

Checking on me, Janie thought. Keeping an eye on her crazy roommate.

"Wanna come with me, get some real coffee at the Student Center . . . " Susanne's voice trailed off. "Janie, what's happened? What's wrong?"

"It's him!" Janie's voice came out in a hysterical shriek.

"Shh!" Susanne looked quickly around, then dropped her pack on the floor and slid into the seat across from Janie.

"Don't 'shhh' me. I told you and you didn't believe me. Now looked what happened!" Janie shoved the newspaper across the table at Susanne.

Why didn't Susanne look shocked? Horrified? Surprised?

She didn't. Instead she read the article, then said, "What a horrible thing to have happened. Poor man."

Janie said, "It was the wolf."

"It wasn't a wolf. There isn't any wolf. And no wolf or dog would kill like that. Janie, think. Don't you think the police would know an animal bite when they saw it? Don't you?"

Janie pulled the newspaper back across the table and stared down at it. "Maybe."

"Definitely! Come on Janie, be realistic. A wolf bite, any animal bite is totally different from two stab wounds like they describe. Whoever killed the guard was human . . ."

Once again Susanne's voice trailed off. Her eyes met Janie's.

"Two stab wounds," Janie said. "Oh my god, Susanne. Lucas. It's the same person who killed Lucas. He's come back for me!"

Janie jumped up and would have run out of the caf, but Susanne caught her, pulled her back down. "Stop it Janie! Stop it now!" she ordered.

"Why don't you believe me?" Janie whispered. "Why won't anyone believe me?"

"Because it's crazy," Susanne said harshly. "That's why." Whatever happened to the guard had *nothing* to do with you. *Nothing* to do with Lucas's death. It was a stupid, random act of violence. Are you listening?"

Slowly Janie nodded her head. She wanted to believe Susanne. But how could Susanne be so sure?

"You've got to let go of Lucas. He's dead. The police are still looking for his killer. They'll find whoever it was. But you can't wait. You've got to get on with your life. Leave the past behind, Janie . . . before it's too late."

Abruptly, almost as if she was angry, Susanne pushed back from the table. "I've got class," she said. "You coming?"

"No. Not yet. I'm going to . . . finish my coffee."

"Suit yourself," said Susanne.

Janie barely heard her. She stared down at the newspaper. "Two stab wounds to the neck."

Is Susanne right? she wondered. Could it really just be a coincidence? A terrible, terrible coincidence?

"You shouldn't be walking alone."

The voice slid out from the shadows, to be followed, a moment later, by the figure of Jon, in the same tux jacket and dark pants he always wore.

Janie jumped in spite of herself. "What do you want?" she said crossly. It had been a long, hard day. Everyone on campus had talked about nothing else, it seemed, except the murder. And all the waiters and waitresses at the cafe were talking about it, too. Janie had been almost glad that Crystal wasn't working that night, so she didn't have to talk about it with her.

"I'll walk you home," said Jon.

"Don't you ever change clothes?" Janie said. She knew she was being rude, but she didn't care.

To her surprise, Jon laughed. She found herself smiling reluctantly back. "Sorry," she said. "It's been a tough day."

"You work hard. It isn't easy, being a waitress and going to school."

Janie looked back over her shoulder at the cafe. She'd flipped the closed sign over, but Will and Norton were still inside, waiting for a last table to finish. "No," she agreed. "But I like the work."

Then she turned. "How did you know I was a student?"

Jon pointed. "You're carrying a Salem U backpack, among other things. Like the books that you study when you're sitting at the counter."

Flattered at his attentiveness in spite of herself, Janie took a tentative step forward to join Jon. He held out his arm, flashing her a quick smile.

She reached out to take Jon's arm and a voice said, "Hey, Janie, over here!"

"Stretch?"

"I called and Susanne said you might need a ride home tonight."

"It sounds wonderful," she said, forgetting all about Jon. "My feet are killing me."

Jon said, gently, "Maybe another time."

"Oh!" Janie turned to him, her cheeks flaming. "I'm sorry. I didn't mean to be rude. Would you like a ride, too?"

Jon shook his head, fading back in the shadows. "Get home safe," he said.

"Bye," she answered. She blinked. How had he done that, melted away so quickly, so quietly?

"Janie?" Stretch's voice said, and she forgot about Jon. She hurried toward the car.

They didn't talk much on the way home. Janie suspected that Susanne had told Stretch all about the previous night. She was sorry for that. She would have liked to have talked to Stretch, to tell him about everything that had been happening herself. But if Susanne had been telling him things, what chance did she have of him believing her?

If Susanne really wanted me and Stretch to be closer, Janie thought, she'd stop interfering.

"Here we are," said Stretch, interrupting her thoughts. He faced Janie. "I was wondering, you know, if we could go out again."

"You really want to?" Janie asked, in spite of herself. "I mean, after what happened?"

"It was just one of those things," Stretch said.

Janie caught herself before she laughed aloud. Just one of those things? Being attacked by wolf — or thinking you were being attacked by a wolf — was just one of those things?

Instead she just smiled and said, "Okay, then. Let's try again."

"Cool!" said Stretch. "I'll call you."

"You do that," Janie agreed. She leaned over and gave Stretch a quick kiss on the lips. She sensed, rather than saw him blushing as she jumped out of the car.

Stretch watched her as she ran into Quad Main. She didn't look back, but she knew he was there. It made her feel good.

Good old Stretch. If only Susanne wouldn't interfere so much.

But then, of course, there was Bram, too.

Janie didn't look back. And she didn't know how long Stretch sat there, staring at the door she had just gone through.

She might not have called him good old Stretch if she'd seen his expression . . .

Chapter 7

"Mondo weird," said Crystal. "*And* they haven't caught anybody. And get this — there've been reports of an animal howling around Salem U. Like a wolf, you know?"

Trying to ignore Crystal's obsessive chatter about the murder, Janie was suddenly jerked to attention. She stopped so abruptly that coffee sloshed out of the cup and onto her hand. "Oww!"

"You okay?"

"What did you say? About a wolf?"

"That I think it's all tied together, y'know," Crystal explained. "You laugh at me about vampires, but — "

"The howling, Crystal. What about that?"

With an exaggerated sigh, Crystal said, "Some people have reported hearing this weird howling around campus."

"Has anybody . . . seen . . . anything?" Janie asked carefully.

"What do you mean?" Crystal fixed Janie with a surprisingly shrewd look. "Seen like what?"

Janie shrugged. "Well, you know, whatever's making the noise."

Crystal studied Janie for a moment longer, then said, "Nope. But I have a theory. I think it's a vampire. Two stab wounds in the neck. A howling, like a wolf. That's one of the shapes vampires take, you know. They can turn themselves into animals, like wolves."

For one moment, Janie almost believed Crystal. For one moment, she saw the wolf, enormous, supernatural, running alongside her . . . .

Then she shook it off. She had to keep a cool head in all this. Had to stay rational. Or she'd go crazy.

Not that she wasn't going crazy already.

Dating Stretch *and* Bram.

Leading a double life.

As if she were reading Janie's thoughts, Crystal said, "How's Bram?"

"Fine." Janie suddenly smiled. "He's meeting me tonight after work."

"So what else is new?" Crystal teased.

"Doesn't that boy ever take you out by the light of day?"

"He's a night person. I guess I'm turning into one, too," Janie said. It was true. Except that not only was she staying up late, she was getting up early. What was the point of sleeping if all you had were bad dreams? Besides, if she stayed a little tired, she didn't feel things as intensely. Didn't remember as clearly.

Like Lucas. Like Lucas's killer out there still . . .

Like the campus cop, his killer out there, too.

Crystal said, "The night belongs to lovers, babe . . . and here he comes."

Janie smiled and turned. Her shift was ending and Bram was walking through the cafe door, right on time.

She waved good-bye to Crystal and Norton as she left. For a moment, stepping outside the boundary of light cast from the cafe window, she had a sense of uneasiness. Of being watched.

Of being followed.

But when she looked around, she just saw all the same familiar objects: cars, shop windows, trees. Nothing new. Nothing frightening.

She climbed onto the Harley behind Bram,

cinched the chin strap of her helmet, tightened her arms around him and whispered, "Let's get out of here."

Who would have ever thought that Stretch and Max would be hanging out in a pool hall that had a row of motorcycles parked out front? They were basketball players. Wasn't staying out late in bad company against the rules?

For a moment Janie, looking up from a shot she was lining up, wanted to run. Instead she forced herself to keep her hand steady.

She missed the shot.

She put her pool cue down with a smile at the guy she was playing. "Good game," she said.

"Maybe next time," he answered indifferently.

Bram kissed her on the lips, lightly, and said "I'm gonna get something to drink. You thirsty?"

"Not yet," she said.

She watched Bram move away. She turned to face Stretch and Max as they came up.

"Hi," she said. "What're nice boys like you doing in a joint like this?"

Neither of them smiled. Stretch said, "It *is* you."

"Yep," said Janie. "And believe me, I don't always lose."

Stretch motioned vaguely. "What're you doing here?"

"I couldn't sleep," she said. Then seeing the hurt, puzzled misery on Stretch's face, she said, more seriously, "I came here after I got off work. With a friend."

"A friend?" said Max. "Sure."

"Max," said Stretch warningly.

Max snorted. "I'll be around," he said, and made himself scarce.

Janie faced Stretch. "I'm on a date, okay, Stretch? With Bram."

"You never told me about him."

"What's to tell? I like Bram. I like you. I'm not serious with either one of you."

"I know you're not ready for that, Janie, but I was hoping . . ."

Janie's frayed nerves suddenly snapped. "Hoping what? I don't know what Susanne has told you — and all the rest of the world — but the truth is, Stretch, that I just want to have fun. That's all. No commitments. Not now. Not ever again."

Sweet Jane Forever. The words came unbidden to her mind. She pushed them away.

"So if that's what you were hoping for, go

find yourself some other girl. Some nice, sane, normal girl. Some girl who didn't find her boyfriend murdered!"

Janie grabbed her pool cue as if she were going to use it for a weapon — to fend off Stretch or all the rest of the threatening world, she wasn't sure.

A voice said, "Hey, I can't leave you alone for five minutes; you're starting a pool hall brawl." Bram's hand closed over the stick and over her hand.

"Bram," she said. She took a deep breath. "Meet Stretch. Stretch, Bram."

Stretch gave Bram a hard look. Bram didn't seem to notice. He smiled. "Shoot a game?" he offered.

"No. I was just leaving," Stretch said shortly.

Bram shrugged and sauntered over to the cue rack to pick out a cue.

"Stretch . . . let's just let things go for a while," Janie said. She couldn't bear the misery on Stretch's face. But it was better to do this now than wait.

"Are you sure?" Stretch said.

There was such pleading, such anguish in his eyes that she almost relented. Almost.

"Yes, I'm sure."

Unexpectedly, Stretch reached out and touched her cheek softly. "I understand," he said.

He turned and left the pool hall. Janie raised her hand to her cheek wonderingly. The touch of Stretch's finger had been like an electric shock.

How had he done that? She could feel the tingle through her whole body.

"Stretch," she whispered softly. But she didn't call him back.

"Hello, Cinderella." Susanne looked up from her books. Her expression, Janie noted, wasn't friendly.

"Hi," she said.

"Late shift at Morte par Chocolat?"

"Nope."

Silence. Susanne was waiting for Janie to explain. Just like she's my mother or something, Janie thought.

But she wasn't going to give Susanne the satisfaction. She took off her jacket and hung it on the back of the door.

"Well?" Susanne's word was like a pistol shot.

"Well, what?" Janie spun around. "I'm sure you've already heard reports from your spy network."

Color flamed in Susanne's cheeks. "My *spy* network? Is that what you call my friends? Because if it is, you've got a very sick idea of friendship!"

"Didn't Max call you the moment he got home tonight? Didn't he?"

"Yes, but — "

"And I'm sure you've heard his story. So why bother listening to mine?"

"Janie, Stretch is a very nice guy. Good. Honorable. How could you do that to him?"

"Do what? Date someone else? Stretch and I went on one date. He doesn't own me! And neither do you."

"Janie!"

Janie grabbed her jacket from the hook on the back of their dorm room door and shrugged it back on.

"Janie!"

Yanking open the door, Janie spun around. Her eyes were blazing, her voice low and venomous. "You don't like Bram. You don't think he's good enough for me. You don't think I should be serious about him.

"Well, that's what my parents said about Lucas. And Lucas is dead. Is that what you want, Susanne? To kill everything that I like that you don't? Well, you're not going to. You don't run my life. So go get a life of your own!"

As Susanne gasped and sputtered in rage, Janie stormed out, slamming the door behind her. She ran through the halls of the Quad and out of the dorm, not caring how late it was, hardly seeing where she was going. As she ran images flashed before her eyes: Susanne and Janie as kids, Susanne always in charge, always the boss; Susanne's face when Janie had told her about Lucas — about dating him, about his murder — the horrified disbelief, Lucas dead.

Dead. Dead.

As dead as her heart.

She ran and ran, until she couldn't run anymore. She ran until the images were a blur. Until the only thing she could hear, the only thing she could feel, was the pounding of her heart.

At last she stopped. She bent forward, her hands on her knees, gasping for breath. Where was she?

A huge old building towered above her on the right. She frowned, straightened up and looked around, getting her bearings. For one awful moment, she thought she'd run too far, that she had run, somehow, all the way to Nightmare Hall. She imagined the dead girl standing at the door, holding out her hands, calling Janie in.

No. That couldn't happen. And anyway, new people were living in the old dorm now. Nightmare Hall was just a nickname.

But she was, she realized, standing in front of an old dorm. An old *empty* dorm. Abbey House. It had been part of the campus since the beginning, an old women's residence hall. Now it was only used for conventions and conferences and for special visitors.

She turned to go home, her rage spent. She was exhausted. She'd never been so tired in her life.

And then she heard it. In all the silence of the night, the whisper of a footstep.

She froze, her eyes straining to penetrate the darkness. Nothing moved.

"Hello," she said. The word came out as a plea.

No one answered.

Then she heard it again.

The wolf, she thought wildly, confusedly. The murderer.

The vampire.

Turning, she ran with the last of her strength toward the shelter of Abbey House.

Chapter 8

She flung herself against the door of Abbey House, twisting to put her back against it, to face her pursuer.

A shadow moved at the edge of the walk leading up to the dorm.

The door gave way. With a gasp of surprise, she fell inside.

In an instant she was scrambling to her feet. She slammed the door hard and stopped in the darkness. Dim light came from the windows — just enough to see the stairs ahead. Without giving herself time to think, she flung herself forward and dashed up them.

The pounding of her footsteps didn't drown out the sound of the door opening below.

She turned at the top of the stairs. "Go away!" she shouted. "I know who you are! You won't get away with this."

No one answered still. All she could hear was

the sound of her own labored breathing.

And then the footsteps crossing the floor below.

Janie turned and fled. Down the long dark row of dorm rooms, her fingers trailing on the wall to keep her from crashing into it.

Then her fingers met air. She swung wildly and almost toppled forward over the railing of the stairs at the far end of the hall. She stopped herself.

She looked over her shoulder.

Into a tunnel of darkness.

With a sobbing breath, she ran down the stairs. She skidded out onto the first floor landing and almost fell. She ran back toward the front door.

She was almost there when some instinct stopped her.

He was there. By the door. Waiting.

She didn't know how she knew, but she did.

She swung into the opening at her right, the old-fashioned formal reception room of the dorm.

It wasn't a big room, but it was filled with ancient, heavy furniture. For a moment, she thought of hiding behind a couch, a chair. But it seemed so obvious.

He was behind her. Coming after her. She leaped forward and slid behind the heavy curtains that framed the window. She willed herself not to breathe.

The steps were as soft and faint as the footsteps in a dream. They were hardly footsteps at all, so lightly did he tread.

And then she heard the voice. The sweet and deadly whisper.

"Janie . . . Sweet Jane . . ."

She screamed as she had never screamed before in her life. And ran blindly out from behind the curtain.

Something touched her hand, a cold and icy hand. She lashed out wildly and plunged forward, screaming, screaming, screaming . . .

The front door smacked against her outstretched fists, bruising her knuckles. It burst open and she fell into the greater darkness of the night.

Hands grabbed her.

"Nooooo!" she moaned. "Nooooo!"

"Janie? Shhh. Janie . . . it's me. Bram."

She shuddered convulsively, then fell limply against his shoulder.

"Janie? What's going on? Are you okay?"

"Get away," she murmured. "Water . . ."

"Can you walk? There's a water fountain up at the Student Center. We can stop there . . ."

She nodded numbly and allowed Bram to lead her away from the building. She was safe now. Whatever it was wasn't after her anymore.

Bram had scared him away.

At the fountain she drank as if the water were life itself. She splashed some of it on her hands and face and began to feel slightly better. But her knees were still weak.

"Can we sit down for a minute?" she asked.

"My thoughts exactly," Bram said, motioning to two chairs at one end of the terrace surrounding the Student Center. "In fact, I've managed to save us two seats."

It was a weak joke, a silly thing, but it made her smile. Leaning on Bram, she headed for the chairs and sank down gratefully into one of them.

"Now," said Bram, keeping her hand in his as he sat down next to her, "suppose you tell me just exactly what is going on."

Could she tell Bram the truth? Or would he think she was crazy? He sat quietly, unmoving, waiting patiently for her to begin. For a moment, she felt with Bram as she had felt with Stretch: that he was solid, a rock she could lean on.

Maybe it was true. Maybe beneath Bram's brooding exterior, his conceited posturing, there was a real, sensitive person, someone she could depend on.

Someone she could trust.

She took a deep breath. "It began in high school," she said quietly. "It began with a boyfriend. Lucas."

To her surprise and relief, Bram never interrupted her while she was talking, never exclaimed aloud in surprise and disbelief. When she was done, he said simply, "It sounds like you're due for a break. This is all too much for any human being to bear."

"Then you do believe me?"

"Why would you lie?" said Bram. He paused, then said quietly, "Lucas. Did you — love him very much?"

"Yes," she said even more quietly.

"Do you think you'll ever feel that way about someone again?"

She was silent for a moment. Then she said, "Once I would have said no. Never. But now, I don't know."

Bram leaned over and put his arm around her. He held her tightly for a moment, then dropped a kiss lightly on her lips. "It's getting late," he said. "Or maybe I mean early. The sun will be up in a little while. I'd better be getting you home."

He stood up and held out his hand. She stood up too and slid her hand into his. They walked back to the dorm without speaking. When they got there, Bram said, "Go easy on that best friend of yours. She means well."

"I'll tell her you put in a good word for her," Janie said.

Bram chuckled. He kissed her and walked quickly away.

Janie went up to her room and slept the sleep of the dead.

"So are we not speaking today?" Susanne's voice interrupted Janie's thoughts as she sat up sleepily and made a grab for her clock.

"Good grief!" Janie said groggily. "I've got exactly half an hour to get ready and get to my shift at the restaurant."

"Never mind your classes," said Susanne.

"Susanne, cut me some slack here, okay?"

"I was worried sick about you last night," Susanne said, dropping her books on her desk and leaning back against it. She folded her arms in front of her and watched as Janie scrambled desperately into her waitress outfit. "Running out in the middle of the night like that. It's not safe to wander around alone at night at the best of times, but now, in case you haven't noticed, there's a murderer on the loose in Salem."

"Really?" Janie yanked her blouse on and began to button it up. "Gosh. I thought I'd imagined it. Stress and all, you know. After all, my boyfriend was killed and I found the body, so that must make me crazy, right?"

Flushing angrily, Susanne said, "That's not fair, Janie."

"The world's unfair," retorted Janie. "And I'm late." She left before Susanne could answer.

Even though she was late, Janie paused for just a moment outside Morte par Chocolat to peer inside. It was like watching a play, the inside of the restaurant lit up like a stage, while she was the audience, on the other side of the cafe windows.

Funny that a part-time job at a coffeehouse would be the place she'd feel most at home, most comfortable. Being a waitress had never been part of her plans for her glamorous life at Salem U. But it had given her a sense of independence, a sense of responsibility. It had also given her something to do to keep from thinking about Lucas.

To keep from going crazy.

"Thinking of cutting work?" said a velvety voice in the ear.

Janie barely kept herself from jumping in surprise. She kept her attention focused on the scene inside the cafe and answered, without turning her head, "Do you always sneak up on people like that?"

Jon laughed. "Nope." He nodded toward the window. "Nice fireworks."

The sun had just set and the glass was painted with the reflections of its afterglow, fiery oranges and reds. Now the scene inside looked as if it were taking place behind a veil of fire.

Janie drew her breath in sharply at the image, hating it. Not the cafe. The cafe was the one safe place. Crystal, Norton, the customers with their easy, specific demands . . .

"I'm not cutting work," Janie said.

"Aw, come on!" For a moment Jon sounded like an eager schoolboy, not the mysterious stranger, the dangerous figure that Crystal imagined him to be. Janie realized that Jon probably worked very hard at his image, hiding his insecurities behind his dark glasses, shrouding his insecurity in a cloak of secrecy.

When the truth was that he probably didn't have any friends. Neither she nor Crystal had ever seen him with anyone at the cafe. He'd never talked to anybody but the people who waited on him. He was probably just as shy, in his own way, as Stretch.

Janie turned to look at Jon. He looked back at her. He smiled slightly, as if he could read her thoughts.

"Well, I've got to get to work," Janie said. "See you later."

"I hope so," said Jon.

Customers came and went in a steady flow all night. At break, Crystal said, "Yo, Janie, you look asleep on your feet."

"Late night," said Janie.

As Janie had known she would, Crystal leered. "Was it fun?"

"You've got a dirty mind," said Janie.

"Thank you," said Crystal. She nudged Janie with her elbow, then slurped down the rest of her coffee. "That table over there, see? It's going to give me a big tip. I can tell. It's a couple out on their first date and he's trying to impress her."

"You are *sooo* cynical," said Janie.

"Hey," said Crystal, "when you've been around as long as I have, you know."

"Gee, Crys, how old are you?" Janie mocked.

"Ancient," said Crystal. "Practically dead." She made a face. "Being a waitress is killing me . . ." She jumped off her stool, picked up her tray with a flourish, and headed for her victims.

Janie shook her head. The hapless couple

probably would give Crystal a big tip — but it would be because of the force of Crystal's personality, not because the guy was trying to impress the girl.

She looked at her watch. She'd almost finished work for the night. Just two more tables.

Finishing her soda, Janie picked up her own tray. She stopped uneasily. She had the strangest sensation of being watched.

She surveyed the restaurant, half expecting to see Jon in the corner booth, his dark glasses turned her way. But the back booth was empty. Her eyes turned to the front window. Was there an audience out there beyond the light that lit the front of the restaurant and the sidewalk? Was someone watching the people inside the restaurant?

Or was someone out there watching her? A murderer? A chill crept over her.

Crystal swooped by, holding a tray of empty cups and said, "You missed that table by the front door. I grabbed the cups, but it still needs a once-over."

Thanks," Janie said automatically, distracted from her morbid thoughts. She frowned. She was sure she had cleared that table by the door off earlier, right before her break.

"Get a handle on it, girl," she muttered to herself. She hurried across the restaurant toward the offending table.

Quickly she began to wipe the table off with one hand while reaching for a piece of paper on one side of the table. It looked like a letter someone had left behind.

Maybe it was a love letter, she thought. Crystal would like that.

Unsuspectingly she reached down and picked up the letter. She wasn't going to read it, she told herself. Just see to whom it was addressed so it could be returned.

But the words leaped out at her:

Sweet Jane Forever.
Have you forgotten me so soon?
I haven't forgotten you.
I never will.
Sweet Jane Forever.
Mine.

Chapter 9

"Janie! Janie, what's wrong?"

The distant sound of a crash reverberated in Janie's ears. She looked down and realized that she had dropped her tray.

At least nothing was on it, she thought mechanically.

"Nothing," she answered. "Nothing's wrong."

She folded the note with numb fingers and shoved it into the pocket of her jeans. As she did she heard the door open behind her, felt the chill of the late evening wind on her neck. Then a voice said, "I saw what happened through the window. Are you okay?"

"Jon?" Janie turned.

"I came for coffee, but I can walk you home if you'd like."

Crystal said, "I'm giving her a ride."

Jon met Crystal's eyes, then said, "Oh. Well.

Okay." He smiled a little smile and walked over to his usual booth.

"You don't have to drive me home, Crys. I'm okay," Janie said.

"Yeah, yeah, yeah. Now go get your stuff and let's get out of here before Norton decides we should do a double shift."

As if Norton would ever do something like that, Janie thought.

She waited for Crystal and walked with her out to Crystal's car gratefully. Janie could feel the note in her pocket, feel it burning against her leg.

The words seethed in her brain. Huge, slashing, black-inked words.

Lucas's words.

Lucas's handwriting.

But Lucas was dead.

So who could be doing this to her?

Susanne, she suddenly thought. And thinking it, believed it.

Susanne, Susanne, Susanne.

Who else could it be? Who would know Lucas's handwriting well enough to imitate it? Might know his pet name for her?

Who else was angry at her? Who else was acting totally weird?

Susanne

Her best friend. Her oldest, closest, sick, sick friend . . .

"Wanna talk about it?" Crystal offered as she guided her car along the quiet, dark streets of Salem U.

Janie said, "Roommate problems, mostly."

"Boring," said Crystal. "I hate roommates. It's why I crash off-campus, or one of the reasons, anyway . . . but listen, if you want to take some time off from yours, get away, you can always hide out at my place for a few days."

"Even though you hate roommates?"

Crystal shrugged and grinned. Janie was unexpectedly touched.

"Thanks. I really appreciate it. I may take you up on it."

"Well, any time. Y'know? The key is under the welcome mat of my across-the-hall neighbor — he keeps his under mine — and I have a foldout sofa in the giant closet that passes as my living area."

Janie laughed. It wasn't much of a laugh, but it was better than nothing. Then she stopped. Roommate problems? Who was she kidding? This wasn't just your average roommate problem. Susanne was trying to drive her crazy. Make her lose her mind.

Aloud she said, "I may take you up on it sooner than you think."

Susanne wasn't in their room when Janie got back. But Janie wasn't surprised. Of course Susanne isn't here, she thought. She's wandering around campus, spying on me and my friends and leaving horrible notes every time I don't do what she thinks I should do.

Like hang out with Bram. And be friends with Crystal. And although she claims otherwise, maybe she wants me to mourn Lucas forever.

Had Susanne always been like that, so jealous, so controlling? Or had Lucas's death and leaving home to go to Salem just brought out the worst in Susanne?

Sliding into her bed, Janie played the questions over and over in her mind. But she didn't come up with any answers. And her resolve to stay awake until Susanne came home, to have it out with her, faded into sleep before Janie even knew what had happened.

When she woke up the next morning, her roommate had come and gone.

Susanne was avoiding her. Did she know that Janie had figured out what she was up to?

"You can run, but you can't hide," Janie said to Susanne's empty bed.

Then she remembered Crystal's offer. A slow smile curled her lips. Maybe she would take Crystal up on her offer. Like that very night. Maybe she'd let Susanne stew for a few days, really worry.

Then she'd confront her. Really have it out with her best friend once and for all. And if she didn't have a best friend when it was all over, well, too bad.

"Crystal?"

Janie knocked again. No one answered.

Using the key she'd gotten from under the doormat in front of the apartment door across the hall, Janie let herself into Crystal's apartment. She'd been by before when Crystal had given her rides, but she'd never been inside.

It wasn't what she expected. It was very plain. Very neat. Almost like a hotel room, except that the furniture was shabby.

"Crystal?" Janie called again. No one answered.

Janie dropped her backpack and her tote bag with its change of clothes on a director's chair by the one narrow window and went in search of sheets and towels. She found them on shelves above the bathroom door and stood on the edge of the bathtub to get them down.

Crystal hadn't been kidding. Her apartment

was small. Very small. And stuffy. Janie opened the front window a few inches, then went to work on the sofa bed. When she had it unfolded and her things sorted out, she made a sign and taped it to the front door: "Crystal! Don't freak. I'm inside. Janie."

That done, she settled in on the sofa bed to get in some study time.

The minutes ticked by and turned into hours. She listened to the late night sound of traffic on the busy street two stories below Crystal's front window.

After awhile, she grew restless. She went into the kitchen to see if there was anything to eat or drink, but Crystal's fridge and cupboards, like the rest of her apartment, were neat — and empty.

Holding a glass of tap water, Janie wandered around. It was a very impersonal apartment: no photos of family on the dresser in Crystal's bedroom, no funny postcards stuck to the refrigerator with silly magnets, no posters for bands or stars on the walls. Her one bookcase was only half full, and the books that filled it, lined up in alphabetical order, were all schoolbooks — except for the bottom shelf, which was all filled with stories of the supernatural . . . including, Janie noted, a number of books about vampires. Was that Crystal's dark secret? Did she *really* believe in monsters and werewolves and vampires?

Suddenly Janie felt like an intruder. What business of hers was it how Crystal lived? Or that she lived almost like a fugitive, as if she could walk away at any time. . . .

It just proved that Crystal, like Bram, like Jon, wasn't what she seemed. You couldn't judge people by appearances.

Janie took her glass of water and went back to the sofa bed. Far, far away, in the distance, she heard the chiming of the clock tower. It was two A.M. If Crystal had gone in to work that night, which she wasn't scheduled to do, she would be home by now. The cafe closed at eleven on weeknights. Even the late-night study section of the campus library closed at two.

But then, Janie thought wryly, Crystal was hardly likely to be studying at the library. She was probably at some all-night party. She'd come rolling in at dawn full of stories and laughter.

Good old Crystal.

Trying to still the uneasiness that was gnawing at her mind, Janie at last turned off the lamp and went to sleep.

She didn't know what woke her. She came up out of a deep sleep, as if she were rising from the bottom of a well. For a moment she was disoriented, confused. She couldn't remember where she was.

Then she realized that she was at Crystal's, asleep on the sofa bed in her living room.

"Crystal," she said softly, thinking Crystal had come home and that that was what had pulled her up out of sleep. But no one answered.

The sound of traffic outside the window was less. A post-midnight chill had crept into the air. She yawned hugely and sat up to grope for the covers.

Where were they? Annoyed, she reached out and turned on the light and got out of the bed to pick the covers up off the floor.

And froze. It was that sensation again. That sensation of being watched. Of greedy eyes devouring her from the darkness beyond.

Janie turned her head slowly.

A huge rat was standing on the ledge of the partially open window, halfway inside.

It didn't move. Except its eyes. Huge, bloody-red eyes that flamed against the darkness behind it.

I don't believe this, she thought. She took a step back, trying not to panic.

The rat moved. It moved slightly forward. "Who are you?" she heard herself say, sounding shrill and frightened, like a child.

And the voice answered.

Janie, it said.

Sweet Jane . . .

Chapter 10

She opened her mouth to scream.

The rat stood up.

Later she wouldn't remember how she did it, how she leaped across the room, the clock by the bed in her hand, wouldn't remember hurling it at the rat or seeing the rat disappear as the clock shattered against the windowsill.

All she remembered was the moment after, her hands against the window, the echo of it slamming shut still in her ears, the lights of the cars passing below.

The rat was gone.

"Oh my God," she breathed.

She heard the voice again, the faint mocking echo in her head. The old familiar voice.

Lucas.

She looked out into the darkness, but there was nothing there except the reflection of her face in the windowpane.

She was alone. And more afraid then she had ever been in her life.

The morning came without Crystal.

Without sleep. Although she'd closed the window and locked it, although she left the light on, Janie couldn't fall back asleep. She wished Crystal would come home from the party.

She wished she could talk to someone.

But there was no one.

When her watch told her it was time to begin the day, she got up numbly and got ready for class. She took the note off the door when she was leaving, slipped the key back under the doormat across the hall.

She hoped Crystal was okay.

I'm at Crystal's. Please don't call me or let anybody know where I am. I just want to think.

                                        Janie

Janie folded up the note, wrote Susanne's name and box number on it, and dropped it in the campus mail slot in the campus post office. She didn't want to talk to Susanne, but a day passed worrying about Crystal and trying to decide what to do had made her realize that she couldn't let Susanne worry about her the same way. Whatever Susanne had done, it wasn't fair for Janie to do that to her.

She went to her classes and studied for the rest of the day, looking for Crystal on campus and calling her on the phone at her apartment. But Crystal didn't show up for either of her classes. And no one answered Janie's calls.

She thought she saw Stretch once, across the campus, but he turned away when she raised her hand to wave. She looked for Bram, but didn't see him.

Probably, she thought, the bright light of day was too harsh for his eyes. She smiled, realizing that she had never seen Bram during the day. He was the most complete night person she'd ever known.

And she was beginning to turn into one herself. She yawned again and quickly covered her mouth so her professor wouldn't see. In fact, a few more enforced all-nighters and she'd have no choice but to sleep by day.

On the way to work that evening, she stopped and bought all the rat traps on the shelves at the hardware store.

Norton's first words to her as she walked into the cafe that evening weren't reassuring. "Janie! Have you seen Crystal?"

"She's not here?" Janie asked. She looked

around the cafe. Somehow, it didn't seem as safe as it had before.

Norton shook his head. "She had asked for a double shift today. She was supposed to be here two hours ago."

"She hasn't called?"

"Nope." Norton frowned. "It's not like her. She's very reliable. One of the most reliable people I have."

"You haven't called her house?" But she knew the answer before Norton said, "About six times. No answer."

"Something's come up," Janie said firmly.

"Yeah, well I hope it's nothin' bad," said Norton.

Janie watched Norton turn away to make more coffee. I wish he hadn't said that, she thought uneasily. In spite of herself, she looked over her shoulder toward the window.

Where *was* Crystal? What if something terrible had really happened to her?

No, Janie told herself finally. No no no. Then she thought, if she doesn't come home tonight, I'm calling the police.

Because there was a murderer out there.

A murderer. Or something worse.

Or was this all part of some fiendish payback by Susanne?

Norton rang the order bell and she shook

her head, trying to clear it. "Get to work," she told herself firmly.

The key was under the mat where she had left it. Janie bent to pick it up and turned to go into Crystal's apartment.

She touched the key to the lock and the door swung silently open.

A gash of light fell across the doorway into the darkness of the apartment.

"C-Crystal?" Janie said.

Something inside moved.

"Crystal?" Janie pushed the door wider.

"Help me," a voice whimpered.

"Crystal!" In a panic, Janie flung the door open and reached for the light.

For one moment, as the light came on, two figures appeared, like the gruesome actors in a horror play: Crystal, stretched out across the cushions of the sofa, covered with blood.

And him. A huge, towering creature in black. A monster made of shadows and ice.

A predator.

A murderer.

"No!" screamed Janie. "NOOOOOOOO!"

She jerked back and felt the door slam shut behind her as it leaped across the room toward her. Foul air brushed her face.

The lamp crashed to the floor and the room was plunged into darkness.

For one long moment he hung there, silhouetted against the open window, the folds of his coat swirling around him like vast wings.

His eyes blazed red in the darkness.

Then he was gone.

Huddled in a blanket, trembling, Janie watched as the paramedics lifted the stretcher into the ambulance. Crystal, beautiful, animated Crystal, was so still. So silent.

Janie couldn't see her gashed hands and wrists. Wiped clean of blood and bandaged, she lay beneath the blanket drawn up over her still form. But the bandages at her throat were still bloody and the paramedic who bent over her body as she was lifted into the ambulance kept the pressure on the worst of the gashes to slow the bleeding.

"Can I go with her?" Janie asked no one in particular.

"We're contacting her parents now," said a voice. Janie turned. A police officer was standing next to her.

"Detective Chang," the officer said. "You are Janie Curtis?"

Janie nodded.

"I think it might be best for you to get home and get some rest . . . Why don't my partner and I take you back to your dorm. We'd like to ask you a few questions on the way."

Again Janie nodded.

At least it's an unmarked police car, Janie thought as she got out of the car outside the dorm. At least the whole dorm won't know.

"Janie," said Officer Chang as Janie got out of the car.

Closing the door, Janie stopped, staring down at her feet. She'd told the police everything she knew. That she had come home. That the door had been open. That she didn't recognize whoever it was.

That she hadn't even seen his face.

"Is there anything else you want to tell us?"

Janie remained motionless. Yes, she wanted to say. Yes. It's me. It's me he's after. He killed Lucas. He killed that guard. He tried to kill Crystal because he knew I was staying there.

He's a monster.

He's trying to kill me.

"Janie?" Officer Chang prompted.

Janie shook her head and ran up the stairs into the dorm.

* * *

She pretended to be asleep when Susanne came home. She heard the door of the room open, sensed Susanne standing in the doorway of the room. "Janie?" Susanne whispered softly.

She tensed, fearing that Susanne would try to wake her up, try to talk with her. Janie forced herself to take deep, even, slow breaths.

Apparently Susanne was convinced. She tiptoed into the room, and got ready for bed quietly. Not long afterwards, her own deep, even breathing matched Janie's.

But Janie didn't sleep. The images of the night kept flashing before her eyes, vivid bloody images superimposed on earlier images:

Lucas dead, his throat bloody and pierced.

The guard, walking into the darkness where a wolf waited.

Crystal's torn hands and wrists, the gashes in her throat. "She put up quite a fight," one of the officers had said, matter-of-factly. "Saved her life . . ."

Had Crystal fought off a monster?

It was almost as if her obsession with vampires were coming true. Almost as if a vampire . . .

No. It was impossible. There was no such thing as a vampire. The monster who stalked her, who had hurt Crystal, was human. Monstrously human.

Still, the idea took hold. She needed more information. Well, she knew where to find it. But that would have to wait until the next day.

For the second night in a row, she didn't sleep.

"I need to get some books out of Crystal's apartment. I left them . . ." Janie let her voice trail off pleadingly.

A long silence followed. Then Officer Chang's voice said, "We'll have a patrol officer meet you there in half an hour. He will supervise you. Do not touch anything except the books you left. The officer will log them out."

"Thank you," said Janie.

"And if you have anything else you want to tell us," Officer Chang said.

"I'll call you. Of course." Janie hung up the phone, grabbed her pack, and made a quick exit from her room.

It wasn't comforting reading. Nightmare bedtime stories. Janie had taken refuge in one of the study lounges in the basement that ran beneath the Quad, a vast interconnecting warren of hallways and laundry rooms, study rooms and television rooms. The room she'd chosen to spend her afternoon in was small and quiet — but not too far from the comforting noise of some students watching videos in one of the television rooms.

She was glad she had.

Vampires, she read, *can change shape and form. Their preferred animals are wolves and bats and rats, whom they can also command to do their bidding, as they can command some humans within their thrall.*

They travel only at night, fearing the light of goodness and day. They fear also their own reflections in the mirror and command the mirrors to cooperate. A true vampire will show no image in a mirror, nor, some say, in a photograph or any film.

They kill their victims by piercing their throats and draining the blood from their bodies, the blood of humans being the most desirable.

No one knows their origins, the seed of their dark past. Some believe that they give birth rarely and dangerously; that vampires born of vampires are the most powerful vampires of all, the true immortals.

It is said that the true immortals make others like them by draining away their blood in a secret and special way. This is called by some the Vampire's Kiss. Others believe that any vampire, made or born, may give the fatal Kiss. No one knows why the vampires give the Kiss of Death, which means immortal torture and denies the victim the peace of honest death. Perhaps they are lonely . . .

Some say that murders unsolved are the domain of the vampire. That if a person is murdered and the murderer never caught, the vampire can call that person into its eternal night.

Therefore it is best not to let murders go unsolved or unavenged, lest you do the work of vampires.

Yet to catch the vampire is not to kill it.

To kill a vampire you must drive a stake through its heart, the most dangerous of enterprises. For they are immortal strong, immortal quick of hearing, immortal sharp of sight, sharing those attributes with the animals they most favor. Nor can you rely on the charms to ward off the Creature, not garlic nor any charm, except this. If you are inside, you must let the vampire in. It cannot come in uninvited. But for all of that, beyond the stake in the heart, no one knows of any other way to kill a vampire.

"Oh my God," Janie whispered. She leaned her head against her hand and realized that she was sweating. She got up and went to the vending machines and bought a soda with shaking hands. She barely tasted it. Her thoughts spun. She felt sick. Faint.

Crystal had been right. A vampire had been stalking the campus. A real vampire.

More real than Crystal realized.

She pulled her backpack toward her and found the notes. She spread them out side by side on the table.

Sweet Jane Forever.

Forever.

Lucas, she said aloud. And saying it, understood it all.

Lucas was a vampire.

And he had come back for her.

Chapter 11

In numb disbelief, Janie gathered up the books and took them to her room.

She noted vaguely that Susanne hadn't been back.

Then stopped.

Susanne. Was Susanne in the vampire's thrall? Susanne who had dated Lucas once, who had been his "good friend" after he started dating Janie. After he and Janie fell in love.

Was Susanne helping Lucas? Helping him keep others, like Bram, away from her? Was that why Susanne had liked Stretch so much? Because she knew he wasn't Janie's type, knew he was safe . . .

Susanne . . .

Pulling her waitress clothes on in a panic, she fled the dorm.

* * *

"You didn't have to come to work," Norton said.

"Yes, I did," Janie said. She met Norton's eyes, saw the real concern in them, and forced herself to smile. "It's best to keep busy."

And stay around people you can trust.

She added, "Crystal's in a coma."

Norton nodded. "I called the hospital. They've got a police guard on her, too . . ." Seeing Janie's stricken look, he said quickly, "But I'm sure it'll be all right. They'll find the guy who did it, don't you worry."

How much did Norton know? Janie wondered. Her name had been mentioned in many of the news reports about the attack. She didn't ask. Whatever Norton knew, he was too tactfull, in his own weird Norton way, to say anything.

Taking their cue from Norton, the other staff members of Morte par Chocolat only murmured words of sympathy and offers of help, then left her to her job.

She worked hard. Fast. Intensely. She forced herself to concentrate on the job at hand. She was concentrating so hard that she didn't even realize that Bram had come in until he slid onto the stool at the counter next to her while she was sitting there, adding up a check.

"Bram!"

"Janie. I heard about Crystal. You okay?"

"Yes," Janie said and to her horror heard her voice break. "No."

Bram said, "I can't stay here. I just stopped by to see how you were doing. I called your room and Susanne said you'd probably gone to work. So you want me to meet you after work? Give you a ride home? A shoulder to lean on?"

After work. She hadn't even thought that far ahead.

After work. The long walk home after work.

She raised her head slowly. Lifted her gaze from the column of figures she'd been adding up. A thought squeezed itself into her chaotic, frightened mind. A plan.

"Janie?"

"Bram," she said. "Thanks. Maybe another night."

Bram looked at her sharply. "Are you sure?"

She smiled, making her smile convincing. "Can we get together tomorrow? I'd like that."

It worked. Bram gave her a slight smile back, then squeezed her shoulder. "Sure . . . take it easy, then. Tomorrow."

"Tomorrow," she echoed.

Jon had the evening paper open on the table in front of him. Crystal's photograph, taken from her high school yearbook, peered out from the front page.

Janie winced as she put his coffee down.

Jon looked up. The cafe lights glinted off his shades. Once Janie would have smiled. Once she would have joked about it with Crystal.

Now it just seemed silly. A silly boy's attempt at mystery.

"Anything else?" she asked wearily.

"Is Crystal going to be okay?" Jon asked, indicating the paper.

"I don't know," she said. "Anything else?"

But he was oblivious to the brush-off. "Do you think it was the guy who killed the guard? That's what the paper is saying."

"I don't know," she repeated.

Jon said, "I do. Most killers have patterns, you know. When they kill, they use the same method over and over. Slashers. Stranglers."

"Jon, could we not talk about this?"

Jon got it that time. Instantly contrite he said, "I'm sorry. That was so stupid of me . . . Listen, do you want me to wait around and walk you home after work? I mean, I know you get off late and with all this going on . . ."

Janie shook her head and forced herself to smile at Jon. "Thanks," she said. She looked up from her order pad and out the window of the cafe for a moment, then back down to the twin mirrors of Jon's glasses.

"Thanks. But I'm meeting someone."

"Janie?" Norton's voice echoed through the back of the restaurant. He was waiting to lock up the front door.

"Just a minute," she called. She bent over the box and gave the wooden slat one last pull. And it was free. She tucked the jagged piece of wood in the waistband of her pants, buttoned her vest so the top of it didn't show. Then she snagged the flashlight from the shelf. "Okay," she shouted up to Norton. "I'm ready."

She walked along Pennsylvania Avenue. She didn't hurry. She stopped to look in the darkened windows of the shops. She jingled that night's tips in her jacket pocket and tried to think about spending the money on the books and CDs and clothes on display in the different stores.

I should send Crystal some flowers, she thought. Or maybe something more practical. Maybe I'll just take her something when she can have visitors.

She made herself think of Crystal getting better. Made herself think of tomorrow as just another day. A day that would come for her just as it came for everybody else.

But in spite of herself the thought emerged: how did vampires count their days?

How did Lucas count his? She tried to imagine him sleeping, in some dark and hidden place, a graveyard, the basement of an ancient empty house.

Or did vampires sleep in more modern quarters these days? Scientifically darkened rooms, with special alarms?

She stopped in front of a travel agency. "Come Play In the Sun," the sign above a dozen brochures about island vacations proclaimed.

Did Lucas miss the sun? Unbidden, she remembered one of the last days they'd spent together.

They were on a picnic, watching the sunset. Pizza and soda and a blanket on the bay shore near their town. The sun set over the rocky coast on one side, and the moon, a slice of a moon, rose on the other.

Lucas kissed her. And she held onto him fiercely. "They'll never separate us," she vowed. "I won't let them."

"Forget them," Lucas had whispered in her ear. "We can outlast them. We've got a whole future together. Beginning now."

Did Lucas remember? Did vampires keep their human memories, their human feelings?

Or did those drain away with the blood of their human life?

She turned and walked on, hardly noticing the people she passed.

The gates of Salem University loomed ahead. She walked through and stopped.

The globes of the lights that lined the campus walks seemed to bob like buoys on a sea of darkness ahead. She rubbed her eyes. She had to keep herself focused, had to remember what she must do.

She couldn't turn back. She couldn't fail.

She chose her path and walked forward.

The darkness closed around her as she stepped off the walk and cut across the dark heart of the campus. The science building loomed above her.

Slowly, she told herself. Slowly.

Footsteps . . .

Footsteps echoing her own. But light steps. Quick ones.

She reached her goal. A corner where two of the brick walls enclosing the campus met. The walls were high and solid.

She knew from Crystal's book that vampires could scale walls. But they couldn't walk through them.

She walked into the dark corner and turned and pressed her back against it.

And waited.

He came out of the darkness, as she knew he would. Huge, shadowy.

"Come," she said aloud. "Come to me."

The shadow walked forward. Closer. Closer. She raised the flashlight and turned it on.

"Bram!" she gasped.

"Hey, you're blinding me, kiddo." Bram threw up his hands, shielding his eyes.

"Bram," she said in disbelief. *"Bram?"*

"Who were you expecting?" Bram asked. He stepped toward her.

"Stay right there!" she ordered.

"What are you talking about?"

"I know who you are. I know *what* you are."

Bram said, "I'm Bram. I was worried about you. I decided to come back and see if I could take you home after work. And it's a good thing I did, too. Are you out of your mind, wandering around campus like this with a lunatic on the loose?"

"Good try, Bram, but it won't work."

"What won't work?" said Bram.

A voice said, "The game's over, fella."

The flashlight jerked in Janie's hand. "Stretch?" she gasped. It was insane. It would have been funny if she hadn't been so scared.

Stretch nodded simply. "I called. I heard about Crystal. Susanne told me you were at work. So I waited for you. I knew you didn't want to see me, but I wanted to make sure you were safe."

He swung to face Bram and his voice hardened. "And that's when I saw *him* following you."

"Hey, relax big guy," Bram held out a placating hand. "I'm not looking for a fight."

But Stretch didn't seem to hear. He advanced on Bram, his fist clenched. "You," he said through gritted teeth.

"Stretch!" shrieked Janie. "Stop it! He's not what you think he is! He's . . ."

"I know what he is," Stretch said. "You think I don't?"

Bram suddenly laughed, a low, feral growl. "You want to fight? Is that what you want?"

The punch came out of nowhere, lightning fast and vicious.

"Ooof!" Stretch staggered back, clutching his stomach. But as Bram leaped on him, his fist came up to meet Bram's chin.

"Stop it! Stop it!" Janie screamed.

Bram dodged back. He wiped his face. There was blood on his hand.

He looked down at the blood and smiled. "Blood," Bram said softly. As Stretch leaped toward him again, he stepped neatly to one side and brought his hand down once, hard.

Stretch dropped like a stone. Bram started toward Stretch's fallen body.

Forgetting her fear, forgetting everything, Janie hurled herself onto Bram's back. She heard his startled exclamation, felt him stumble.

Then she was falling, twisting and tumbling.

And then everything was still.

Shaken, she rolled over slowly and got to her feet. Two fallen bodies lay in the crazily tilted angle of the flashlight.

She got up and went over and picked it up.

Bram lay still, a bruise already purpling his forehead. Janie said, "Bram?"

He didn't move. But the light next to his head showed a rock partially buried in the dirt and leaves.

She switched the light over to Stretch. He was pale and motionless. "Stretch," she gasped, "Oh, Stretch."

Running to him, she knelt down and lifted up his head. "Are you okay?"

Stretch's eyelids fluttered. "It'll be all right," Janie whispered. "It's me, Janie. I'm here. I'll take care of you."

She wasn't sure, but she thought a faint smile touched Stretch's lips. Carefully she laid him back down again, trying to think what to do.

And Bram groaned.

He was still alive.

Alive.

She got up and went to kneel beside the fallen vampire. He seemed smaller in the flashlight beam, splayed there on the ground.

He groaned again.

She felt the wooden stake digging into her ribs. She looked down at Bram's pale face. She knew what she had to do.

She put her hand on the hilt of the stake.

"I'm sorry," she whispered. "I'm so sorry..."

A voice spoke from behind her. "How touching. How absurdly touching."

Kneeling there, Janie froze.

"What a brave little girl you are. And what a popular one," the voice went on.

Lucas's voice.

Lucas.

"Sweet Jane," the voice said.

Janie spun around.

"Stop right there," she said. She was surprised to hear how firm her voice sounded. How unafraid.

He stopped. She raised the flashlight slowly, slowly up the tall, thin figure dressed in black. In black pants and black boots and a curiously formal white shirt and an old black tux jacket with the sleeves rolled up.

"*Jon?*" she said.

"Sweet Jane," Jon said. He reached up and took his sunglasses off.

And the face that looked back at her became, as she was looking at it, Lucas's face.

Lucas's dead face.

"Nooooo," she moaned, the tears starting to her eyes.

"Tears?" Lucas smiled. The tips of fangs at either corner of his mouth glinted beneath his thin-stretched upper lip.

Then the smile was gone. "Tears, Janie? You cried when I died. But you forgot me so fast. So fast."

"I didn't forget you," she whispered. She couldn't take her eyes off his face. It was Lucas and yet — not Lucas. His skin was pale and waxen. He'd always been still, quiet. But now he was — lifeless. His eyes were dark and flat, like the eyes of a shark. A predator.

A dead thing.

"Lucas," she whispered, in disbelief.

He tilted his head, as if he were considering something. Then he looked at her and a tiny flame of red burned in each eye.

"Do you still remember me, Janie love? Do you still miss me? Will you miss me always?"

"Yes," she said simply.

The vampire raised his head. The flame died

a little in his eyes. "Janie," he said, and this time it was the voice she remembered, Lucas's voice, tender, caressing, kind.

"Oh, Lucas," she whispered.

"I was waiting for you,' Lucas said softly. "I looked up at the sky. It was a beautiful night, a perfect night and I was thinking of you . . .

"And he came out of nowhere and he killed me. He was so strong. So fast. I didn't even have time to think. I remember that one moment I was standing there, looking up at the sky and then I was lying on my back. I was trying to look at the sky, trying to see . . ."

Silent tears coursed down Janie's face.

Lucas went on. "And then you were there beside me. I could hear you, but I couldn't move. I could hear what you said, and I couldn't answer, couldn't tell you that I was sorry, that I hadn't meant to lie to you about loving you forever . . .

"Then you went for help. And *he* was bending over me again. He whispered in my ear, " 'You should never tell a lie. Let's see if she means it, that word that humans use so easily. Let's see if she understands what forever means.' "

Turning his head to one side, Lucas pulled the collar of his shirt down. There on the pale, marble-white flesh were two red scars.

"He put his teeth to my neck once more . . ."

Lucas looked up and the flame leaped back into his eyes. "Do you know what it's like, Janie, this hunger? This need? It is — inhuman. Unbearable . . . I hoped at first they would catch him, and that would put an end to my misery." Lucas laughed bitterly. "But he was gone. He did what he'd done to me, for entertainment or spite or on an inhuman whim, and left me.

"Left me a vampire."

The word hung between them in the night. Lucas laughed again, a cruel, mocking sound. "You don't like to look at me when I say that word, do you? It repels you. I repel you. You want me to go away. . . ."

"No!" cried Janie.

The flames leaped up in Lucas's eyes and Janie realized what she had done. She'd invited the vampire to her.

He smiled. "So you love me still, Janie. I followed you on those dates, you know. At first I was going to try to contact you, to talk to you. Then I decided to frighten all those other *pretenders* away." He gestured toward the motionless bodies of Bram and Stretch.

"Then that security guard cornered me. Actually called me to him, as if I were a dog."

"You killed him," Janie said.

Lucas said, "I did him a favor. I let him die. That was more than was done for *me*."

He stepped closer. Janie shrank back.

"Then I realized that I couldn't let you go like that. I couldn't leave you. I couldn't let you leave me. I made you a promise Janie, remember?"

"That you would love me always," Janie said through trembling lips. "That we would be together forever."

"And now I can really keep that promise. I can give you the gift of eternal life."

"But you're not alive, Lucas! You're dead! You're not human, you're a vampire. And a murderer! You killed that guard. You tried to kill Crystal . . ."

"She guessed. Under that airhead blonde hair, she's got a brain, Janie. You're friends with her. You should know that. She figured it out. She tried to stalk me. *Me*! As if she could stop me. Kill me."

"Will she — be a vampire, too?"

Lucas said, "No. I didn't have time to kill her. Or to give her the Vampire's Kiss. Besides, you're the only girl I'd ever do that for."

He swooped toward her. Janie fell back.

"Lucas, no. NO!" She hurled the flashlight at him and scrambled back. Her shoulder bumped against the wall, and she raced along the wall to the corner.

She wedged herself in and turned to face the vampire.

He was upon her. Closer than she had realized. Moving with supernatural power.

His arms opened above her.

She felt the stake dig into her ribs beneath her heart. With one last, desperate motion she pulled it free and held it up in front of her, clutched tight in her trembling hands.

"Lucas, no. Stop. Stop or I'll . . ."

He hit the stake. She felt it jar beneath her hands, felt it twist.

In horror she let it go. "Lucas!"

He staggered back. He fell to his knees in the beam of the fallen flashlight. He looked down in surprise at the stake, driven neatly into the front of his shirt.

He looked up and the flame leaped up in his eyes until they were consumed with red.

"Lucas," she said.

"It's not a fatal wound," he said. "But very close. A good try, Janie. How you humans fight death . . ."

"Oh, Lucas . . ." Not knowing what she did, Janie stepped forward. She put her hand out. Her fingers touched the marble cheek.

At the touch of her hand, the flame died in

his eyes. "Janie," he said. "Janie."

He looked down at the stake. "There's a note in my pocket," he said. "I wrote it after I killed the guard. It's a confession. A nice human confession, full of remorse. How I killed the guard. Attacked Crystal. I said I was obsessed with you and followed you here."

"Lucas . . ."

Tears scalded her face. She couldn't speak. His hand went up gracefully, dreamily, and took hers. His grip was strong. Frighteningly strong.

She didn't struggle. She watched as he turned her palm over. He pressed his lips to the center of it. She felt the pressure of two sharp teeth against her palm. But they didn't break the skin.

He kissed her palm and raised his head.

He smiled sweetly. "I love you, Janie," he said. "Forever."

Then Lucas let go of her hand. He wrapped both hands around the stake.

And threw himself forward onto it.

And died.

Epilogue

"Welcome back," Janie said.

"Yo, Crystal. You're looking good," said Norton.

Crystal made a face at Norton.

Janie said, "Don't work too hard, now Crystal. We've got you covered, okay?"

Crystal smiled at Janie, as if she'd never been in the hospital in a coma. Crystal was tough, Janie thought admiringly.

But then, she thought, so am I.

No one would ever know just how tough.

The police hadn't liked the story, but they'd had to accept it. Stretch and Bram had followed Janie, worried about her, and with good reason. A maniac was stalking her. There had been a fight (which neither Stretch nor Bram could quite remember clearly) and somehow, the boy they'd called Jon had been killed.

There were no records for Jon anywhere. No

place of residence. No home, it seemed, on earth. He was a drifter, they concluded.

Case closed.

Lucas rested, Janie thought. Wherever he was, he was at peace. Wherever he was, the Lucas she had loved and remembered would always be alive in her heart.

She wondered what had become of the vampire who had attacked Lucas, turned him into a vampire. Would he come back for her someday?

She didn't think so. She wasn't worried. She felt nothing would scare her ever again.

"First customers of the day," Crystal sang out. "Mine or yours?"

Janie turned. Coming in the door was an unlikely foursome: Bram, Stretch, Susanne and Max.

"Janie said you were coming back today," Bram told Crystal. "We came to wish you luck."

Norton leaned over. "Why don't you kids take a break for a minute?" he said. "I can take care of a couple of tables, if any customers show up this early in the day."

"Cool," said Crystal instantly. She sat down at the table and fixed her eyes on Stretch. "Hi," she said in her most seductive voice.

Crystal had never seen Stretch before, Janie

realized. Silent laughter bubbled up inside her as she watched Stretch stare at Crystal.

Janie cleared her throat. "Ah, Stretch?"

He tore his eyes away from Crystal and looked guiltily up at Janie. "It's okay," she said. Stretch blushed as Janie went on, "Stretch, here's somebody I think you should meet. Stretch, Crystal, Crystal, Stretch."

"Hi," said Stretch. He ducked his head shyly.

Janie's eyes met Susanne's in amusement. Clearly Stretch had just gotten over his infatuation with Janie. Susanne rolled her eyes, but she grinned.

"Hey, Max," Susanne said, digging her elbow into Max's ribs, "move over. Let Janie sit next to Bram."

Max said, "I'm getting me an elbow-proof vest, you know that?" But he moved over.

Janie slid into the booth next to Bram. She kissed him lightly on the lips. "Sweet Bram," she whispered softly.

"Forever," he said.

About the Author

"Writing tales of horror makes it hard to convince people that I'm a nice, gentle person," says **Diane Hoh.**

"So what's a nice woman like me doing scaring people?

"Discovering the fearful side of life: what makes the heart pound, the adrenaline flow, the breath catch in the throat. And hoping always that the reader is having a frightfully good time, too."

Diane Hoh grew up in Warren, Pennsylvania. Since then, she has lived in New York, Colorado, and North Carolina, before settling in Austin, Texas. "Reading and writing take up most of my life," says Hoh, "along with family, music, and gardening." Her other horror novels include *Funhouse, The Accident, The Invitation, The Fever,* and *The Train.*

Return to Nightmare Hall . . .
if you dare

Dark Moon

"I hate you!" the teenager cries. The face is scarlet with rage, the eyes dark with fury. "Everyone else is going. Why do you have to be so uptight about everything? You're ruining my life! I wish you would just die!" Sneakered feet whirl, race up the stairs, stomping down upon each riser. The tall, thin figure in jeans and a plaid shirt runs into the bedroom and slams the door, locking it. Hurtling onto the bed, the teenager lies there, face down, furious.

A full moon shines through the window, illuminating the darkness.

The teenager lies prone on the bed for a long time, finally falling asleep, only to be awakened sometime during the night. The head lifts, glancing at a luminescent clock on the bedside table. Quarter past two in the morning.

The moon is now visible through a different window. The figure on the bed rolls over, thinking angrily of being forced to miss the best party of the year. At that moment, a thick, dark shadow slides across the round, pale globe, hiding it as effectively as if someone had just drawn a black velvet curtain over it.

The figure returns to sleep.

The teenager awakens to bright sunshine flooding the room and a breathless hush over the house, and senses instantly that something is not normal. Something has happened. Something is wrong.

There are people downstairs, in the living room, in the kitchen, spilling out onto the wide front porch. Relatives. Neighbors. Friends of the family. All are ashen-faced, with stunned, bleak eyes.

Because something has happened. Something is wrong.

Someone has died.

The mother who was wished dead only the evening before, has obliged — by dying.

Dying during the night, of what the teenager learns in a sympathetic whisper from a relative was a "heart attack". Unexpected. Shocking.

But the teenager knows better. There was no heart attack. The heart stopped beating because it was willed to stop. It stopped beating unexpectedly, for no apparent medical reason, because someone wished that it would. Wished *hard. Wished so hard that the person had summoned up a power they didn't even know they possessed. The power took over and, under the eerie, luminous glow of a full but shadowed moon, made the heart stop beating.*

Didn't mean to. Didn't even know about the power.

But it's too late now.

Still . . . so many parties to go to, so much fun to have — and nothing to stop that now. Nothing to get in the way. The father won't. Doesn't care about things like that. Too busy, too preoccupied, never did have anything to say about it. Only her. *She was the one who ruined everything.*

Won't be ruining anything anymore, will she?

What time did it happen, is the question posed to the father.

He looks stricken. What? Why do you ask? What difference does it make?

What time? *the now-motherless teenager insists.*

"Two-fifteen," the father answers reluctantly. "She made this terrible sound, as if someone had just pounded her in the chest, and it woke me up. I glanced at the clock as I woke up and saw it was two-fifteen. I tried to revive her, but . . ."

Two-fifteen. The very moment that the dark shadow had passed over the full moon.

The teenager would think about that later.

Right now, the thing to do was cry and carry on as expected. It wouldn't be good to let people think there weren't any feelings. Everyone has feelings. Even people with special powers.